I Can't Remember

Alvin Bell

All rights reserved.
First published and printed in the United States of America. No part of this book may be used or reproduced in any manner whatsoever without written permission except in the case of brief quotations embodied in critical articles and reviews.

For information address
Book Writing Experts
445 S. Figueroa Street, Los Angeles, CA 90071
213-289-3888

https://bookwritingexperts.com/

Published by **Alvin Bell**

Printed in the United States

Trent Walker, a successful New York music producer, wakes up in his black SUV. He finds that it's parked not only on the beach but in the water as well...waves crashing against the door is what woke him. He's been shot in one shoulder and is bleeding from a head wound but can't remember how or why it happened.

He can't even remember who he is.

Other Novels by Alvin Bell

No Ordinary Pain

The Impulse of Rage

Prologue

Flagler Beach, just south of St. Augustine, Florida

The day was another scorcher, *hot and irritating, a hundred degrees at least.*

The windows were all down, but the breeze outside seemed nonexistent, almost as if the wind and the breeze from it were standing still…*a still movement, if there's such a thing.*

And then there was the distinct pungent smell and taste of ocean water, *in my nose and mouth, like fish, but salty.*

Also, the constant banging from how hard the waves were crashing up against the side of the SUV I was in, *a combination of it all was no doubt what woke me.*

Although, at any other time, this might've all been welcomed, the sensational sound itself, of the waves, the alluring, charismatic sound of the ocean…*any other time, that alone might've awakened me, but pleasurably.*

However, now, after being awakened suddenly from realizing how close I was to the water, *being in it, actually, was what frightened and scared me half to death. It almost made me jump out my skin after opening my eyes, realizing where I was.*

And not only that, the shirt I had on was ripped and covered in blood. *I'd been shot and could suddenly feel tremendous pain from it.*

My head hurt as well. There was a big knot on it and a cut. A look in the rearview mirror showed that I was bleeding from there too.

But what was even worse and more startling than anything was that I couldn't remember, *not a goddamn thing, how I got there or why.* Even the injuries, nothing that might've explained or suggested why I'd been shot, hit over the head, and left parked so dangerously close to the ocean's edge.

For the life of me, I couldn't remember any of it.

People in hotels along the beach and from high-rise oceanfront apartments were all out on balconies, pointing and looking down at me. And people walking along the boardwalk were starting to gather too, *staring at me sittin' in a black SUV parked in the water thirty feet out from shore.*

The key was still in the ignition. Instinct made me turn it. To my surprise and relief, the SUV started right up, and I was able to at least drive myself out of the water and a few feet further onto a much drier bed of white sand.

The next thing I knew, sirens were wailing, and the beach was flooded and swarming with police cars and officers riding three and four-wheel off-road vehicles. A few lifeguards and law enforcement officers even showed up in boats and on jet skis out in the water, this just before I was passed out again.

It wouldn't be until two days later when I was actually fully awake and coherent, *stitched up, bandaged, and handcuffed to a hospital bed this time, though.*

But still, before two days ago on the beach, I could remember nothing.

***

Three hundred miles away, twelve people, all acolytes to a religious group, faithful followers, gathered and took their seats under what they called and considered *the tree of life,* a big Oak tree, massive in size with limbs that spread up to thirty feet in some places, covering large spans of area.

While awaiting the leader, the thirteenth of the group, voices mumbled and grumbled about a decision that had to be made. An unfavorable decision about whether someone, someone very special and important to them and their group, would live or die.

"Early on in our lives, we were taught that nothing lasts forever, only to find out later that some things do, in fact, last and go on forever, through all of eternity, infinitely," one man said, to make a point.

"Time…it's one of those things…" said one elderly woman, raising a finger, chiming in to share a bit of wisdom and a smile, "…in fact, it's the most precious thing we have, something more important than life itself," she said, in finishing. At a hundred and forty-seven years old, the woman would indeed know a thing or two about time, something that, to her, was definitely an important issue.

And wisdom...well, wisdom was something the woman gained throughout the years and felt somewhat obligated to share.

"Don't forget about the universe," another elderly woman said. This one was a hundred and thirty-two years old and shared a smile as well, a proud smile for the ripe old age she'd lived to see.

"The world of worlds held to arise by and persist through the direct intervention of divine power," the woman said.

"The power of God and all of his creations," another man said, simplifying it yet reminding the woman. He was a hundred and ten years old.

Meanwhile, a flash of lightning, followed by a loud roar of thunder from up above, ignited the night's darkened sky. And then the rain started to fall. Nevertheless, nobody moved; they all remained calm and still as if the rain falling on them was nothing unusual.

"Okay, but evolution is what got us to the point where we are now," said one other gentleman, the youngest of the present group at ninety-eight years old, "...and I think we should continue to have patience and trust the progression. In time everything heals, including our own hurt and pain.

"And so," he added, "Unfortunately for us being human, immortality isn't an option. It doesn't exist except only in our minds or in the memory of others when it comes to us in our departure," he said, standing tall at six foot nine with a head and beard filled with well-groomed salt and pepper hair...still a very handsome man.

"So, it's settled then. The unfortunate circumstances of fate," the first man said, with the rain coming down even harder. He was a hundred and eight with a birthday coming up, a few days away that would make him a hundred and nine years old. "She dies, and the man lives," he said to wrap things up.

The smiles all disappeared, and again the voices mumbled and grumbled in their displeasure.

Chapter 1

In just five years, the RCA Mix Master Production Agency had grown and was now one of the largest record production companies in New York behind only Def Jam, a Russell Simmons company, and Roc Nation, Jay-Z's company.

The expansive growth of Mix Master came due to the recent production of artists like *Mayhem,* the rocker, *Solo Slash,* and white boy *Nic-Spazz,* who had all become multi-platinum-selling rap artists.

The company had recently set sights on another up-and-coming young star, *Wild Boy Reed,* a kid in Miami, supposedly the hottest new rap artist of the south. Signing him could very well take Mix Master Productions right to the very top.

***

Giorgio Giovanni...his father was believed to have been involved with the John Gotti mafia organization as a top lieutenant before being murdered. The money his father left was used to buy the Mix Master Production Company, of which Giorgio was now CEO.

Giorgio sat totally emerged, soaked in the luxury of his own uptown Manhattan office, talking on the phone when Trent Walker, the company's top record producer, walked in. Giovanni kept talking but waved Trent to a chair across from him.

"Angie, I just sent you three grand last week. What did you do with it?" Giorgio asked, his feet up on the desk with the chair he sat in turned at an angle, allowing him a chance to admire the 64th-floor view over Manhattan while talking to whoever it was he had on the phone...Angel Clark, the mother of Ricky, his one and only child.

Angel, aka *Heaven Nevaeh,* Neveah being Heaven spelled backward, or Angie, as Giorgio liked calling her, was an exotic dancer...a stripper who was once the love of Giorgio's life. Giorgio had a thing for strippers, beautiful young women who showed an interest in him. They showed interest not because of how good-looking or charming he was...at thirty-five, Giorgio Giovanni, *the dweeb,* was short, fat, balding on top, and had a bad body build. But he was a millionaire and very generous with money.

On the other hand, Angel Clark was beautiful in every way imaginable. Men adored her, and so did Giorgio, that is, until Angel refused a marriage proposal, *breaking the poor man's heart,* something he never got over.

The two had a son and would remain friends, but the blow to Giorgio's ego was something he would never get over.

Angel said what she had to say on the phone, and then the conversation continued with Giorgio speaking...

"Yeah, well...you can't expect me to keep sendin' money like that either, not just because you wanna go stay at an expensive hotel somewhere. I mean, you get a check from me every month for five fuckin' grand, and you still callin', askin' for more. What the fuck?" he asked after thinking about it. Due to the wild, unadulterated lifestyle she lived, Angel had given Giorgio full custody of their son and promised never to try to get involved with how he was raised. In return, although they were never married and alimony wasn't an issue, Giorgio sent Angel a check once a month anyway, which, as it turned out, never seemed to be enough. He would've complained about it some more if Angel hadn't hung up on him.

"Jesus," he said, after hearing an abrupt *click* on the other end, indicating the call was over.

"Never fall in love with a stripper," he said, turning to give Trent his full attention, "Believe me, they're heartless and way too much trouble."

He was about to say more when the phone rang again. It was Angel calling him right back.

"Okay, send enough so I can get to Miami then, on a train," she added, hoping to sway Giovanni's decision.

"Angie, I'm done with sendin' you extra money. The more I send, the more you want. You'll get the usual five grand a month, but other than that, please stop callin', askin' for more."

"Gee Gee, look...you don't understand. I gotta get outta here, NOW!!!" said Angel, near hysterics, pleading when she shouted at him through the phone, this so he would know how serious the situation was.

"Angie, what's wrong?" he then asked, the agitation in his voice now gone, replaced with concern and worry. He could tell when she was upset or afraid of something. And as much as she got on his nerves, he still cared about her.

"What have you done? Are you in some sort of trouble or danger?"

"Obviously so," he thought after he'd asked. Thinking, *"Stupid question."*

"Gee Gee, look. Just help me get outta here. I'll explain later."

"Okay, where are you?"

"WHY!?! I'm in Philly. Does it really matter exactly where I'm at? Just get me the hell outta here," she said, sounding paranoid about giving him her exact location, another sign of being in trouble or danger.

"Alright, alright...calm down. I've got Trent here in my office. He's about to leave, on his way to Miami. I'll have him stop and get you, and the two of you can ride down together. How about that?" Giorgio asked, thinking it might've been a great idea.

"Okay, that's fine; just tell him to hurry."

"Okay, I will. He's leavin' now."

But, before hanging up the phone, Angel realized that without an exact location or an address, the guy Giorgio was sending wouldn't know where to come to get her. She gave him the address of a friend's house where she planned to be waiting.

The whole time, Trent, sitting in a chair on the other side of the desk across from Giorgio, was left perplexed, wondering, *"What the hell's goin' on with this?"* He knew that Wild Boy Reed was from Miami and that they were trying to find and sign him, but Trent had no idea that he would be the one sent to go take care of it.

And he definitely didn't want any part of babysitting Giorgio's son's mother, *regardless of how beautiful she was supposed to be.* From what he'd heard, she was stunning, very beautiful, but was at the same time nothing but trouble; bad news...a girl who stayed here and there, up days at a time from being high all the time on meth, and sleeping around with whoever, whenever, where ever.

And now she was calling because she'd gotten herself in more trouble.

"It figures," he said, thinking privately in a way characterized by pessimism.

"I know we haven't talked about it yet," said Giorgio to Trent after hanging up the phone, "but I need you to go down to Miami and get this kid signed before some off-brand label starts throwin' money and jewelry at him to get Wild Boy Reed signed with them. On the way, I want you to stop and pick Angie up in Philly. As you might've heard," he said, glancing over at the phone, "she's gotten herself in somewhat of a jam and needs to leave town. Don't ask me what she's done...don't know, and don't care," said Giorgio, throwing both hands up in surrender while raising himself out of the chair.

There was a bar area in one corner of the room. After walking over and pouring himself a shot of gin, Giorgio told Trent, "What can I say? She's my son's mother; that's the only reason I deal with her. Other than that, I could care less," he said, lying to Trent...he still loved her, *"and always will,"* he admitted, but only in thought.

"She wants to go to Miami. So, get her, and take her down with you. Once you're there, drop her ass off somewhere. Oh, and here," he said, pulling a wad of money out from one front pocket. After counting off three thousand dollars, he handed it to Trent. "Give her this, and tell her to call me. And here, fuck it," he said, giving Trent the rest, five or so more thousand dollars, "for whatever else you might need to spend money on," he said, his reason for why he gave Trent the rest.

"Wow..." thought Trent, not about the five grand or so that he'd been given, but about what was supposed to be given to Angel.

"So, she gets the three grand after all," he said privately, confused by it all.

"Why didn't he just send it to her in the first place, like she asked? Oh well," he thought without thinking about it further. *"The life of being a record producer."*

Thirty minutes later, Trent was heading south on I-76 towards the largely regarded historical City of Philadelphia.

Chapter 2

Three days earlier, in Philadelphia, the city of Brotherly Love

At 10:43 AM, Elaine Olamay, the governor's wife and the First Lady of Pennsylvania, arrived downtown at one of the city's nicer banks, the Bank of Philadelphia. She was wearing a brown pants suit, businesslike. She was also strapped with mega diamonds, rings on both hands and ring fingers, along with bracelets, earrings, and so forth, and she was carrying a matching brown portfolio, which all together portrayed class and elegance.

Wealth of the high and mighty was what some would've called it, especially when it came to Elaine Olamay.

Special agents Frank Wheeler, a black former all-American, six foot one, two-hundred-and-thirty-pound tailback at the University of Georgia. And his partner, Todd Marks, a rather tall, six foot six, white, mild-mannered, radical midwestern white guy, both of the FBI. They arrived with her, but in a separate car, behind the First Lady's two SUVs, the one with her in it, and the second one, the one carrying the First Lady's security entourage.

"Wait here...I won't be long," the First Lady said, instructing Tom Hart, the man in charge of security, to have the entourage wait outside while she went inside the bank alone. It wasn't part of normal procedures to allow the First Lady to go anywhere out in public unescorted. But Elaine Olamay, at sixty-two, was the kind of aging, distasteful, high and mighty kind of woman you didn't question or second guess. And usually, as an employee, if she told you to do something, you did it.

"To hell with it. It's about to rain anyway," thought Tom after noticing a mass of dark clouds moving their way. Hurricane season was touching and reminding the country about what time of year it was. And Hurricane Max was skirting the coast, missing actual landfall, but dropping and depositing enough rain and water in some areas to cause flooding.

"They've got security inside the bank. Besides, who other than us is gonna be out in weather like this anyway? She'll be alright," he thought and decided. It's at least what he hoped.

***

The bank had two entrances, one on 42nd Street where the FBI agents and Elaine Olamay, along with her security entourage, had arrived and parked. Another entrance was on Tremble Avenue, the street adjacent to 42nd Street. At 10:50 AM, eight minutes after the First Lady walked in, a blue van arrived at the entrance on Tremble Avenue. Four masked men, all dressed in dark-colored fatigues, and armed with handguns and AR-15-type assault rifles, got out and stormed inside the bank as well.

Once through the door and eight steps up a short marble staircase, the masked men were all inside.

"EVERYBODY DOWN, ON THE FLOOR, NOW!!!" yelled one of them, the one in charge, obviously.

The marble floors and exquisite staircase, along with the huge hanging chandeliers, made the bank look plush and luxurious, more like a ballroom. But make no mistake about it, the men wearing the mask weren't impressed or affected by it. They only cared about one thing—getting in and out as quickly as possible with all the unmarked bills of cash they could carry and steal.

"YOUR MONEY'S INSURED, SO PLEASE, DON'T TRY ANYTHING STUPID, LIKE TRYIN' TO BE A HERO...SUPERMAN DOES DIE, AND SO WILL YOU!!!" the masked man said, after being sure he'd gotten everybody's attention.

They were on a time limit, the masked men. A minute thirty seconds tops, which was all the time they allowed themselves to go in, get the two security guards disarmed, their hands zip-tied with them, then laying on the floor along with all the customers there in the bank...this and getting back out again with all the money.

"Where's the key?" the masked man asked after coming face to face with the bank's manager, a man in his mid to late forties, balding on top, with no desire to be hurt.

But even before the manager had time to respond or answer, the masked man used the butt of the gun to hit the manager hard in the face. If there was any doubt about him cooperating, the doubt was now gone. With a fresh cut on the head and face, a sudden headache, and blood flowing, the manager, now with nervous hands and fingers, quickly produced the key, which was quickly handed off to one of the other masked men.

At about the same time, not that it was something to be worried about, a teller tripped the alarm to notify police about the bank being robbed.

"ALARM ACTIVATED...THIRTY SECONDS!!!" yelled one of the other masked men, the one standing by the door. The whole time the AR15s were aimed and raised in a firing position at all the customers and at the second door, the same door the First Lady used to get in.

Just then, a call came over one of the radios the masked men were carrying.

"We've got company, the 42nd Street entrance. Get out now." It was the driver outside. He'd spotted the First Lady's security team, which had been made aware of the situation inside the bank and was starting to react.

The masked man inside the vault came out in a hurry carrying two large bags filled with cash, one that was passed on to one of the other masked men.

On the way out, backing away, the four masked men then worked in unison, moving quickly but in rehearsed steps and without getting in each other's way.

In less than a minute and a half, the men had all but made it out the door when all hell broke loose outside.

"Two eleven in progress, downtown, 42nd Street and Tremble Avenue at the Bank of Philadelphia."

"Oh shit...the banks bein' robbed," said Special Agent Wheeler, glancing over at Special Agent Marks, who was already starting to open the car door to get out.

The First Lady's security team, all with dark-colored suits and ties on, heard the same dispatch over their radios and got out of the SUVs. With their guns drawn, they were ready to go inside the bank.

Tom Hart was barking orders.

"YOU TWO...TAKE THAT DOOR!!! SMITH AND ME, WE'LL GO AROUND TO THE OTHER ONE!!!"

"NO, WAIT!!!" yelled Special Agent Marks. The FBI was highly trained to deal with bank robberies. But not the security team...they were trained basically to protect and were nowhere near as qualified to respond and handle what might happen in hostile situations of bank robberies.

Neither Tom Hart nor Security Officer Smith saw the driver of the van standing outside between the opened driver's side door and the body of the van with the barrel of an AR15 leveled, pointed, and aimed right at them.

Just as Special Agent Wheeler yelled, "GET DOWN!!!"

Shots were fired, and the two security officers, after being shot, both fell in a heap, dead.

More shots were fired, but the rest of the security team was able to duck and hide, taking cover behind the two SUVs.

After exiting the bank, the four masked men got in the van, and so did the driver before burning rubber to get them all away.

"Anybody else hurt?" Marks asked. There didn't seem to be.

Just then, the door of the bank, there on 42nd Street, burst open, and everybody else inside the bank ran out, including the First

Lady, Elaine Olamay.

"One of the bastards took the damn phone," she said after getting close to Special Agents Marks and Wheeler.

On the way out the door, one of the masked men saw the First Lady on the floor with the phone in her hand. She had it out, recording the scene inside the bank.

"Lady, what're you doin'? Give it to me," he said, with a hand held out.

"You heard me...THE FUCKIN' PHONE!!!" he yelled, bending down to take and snatch it away when the First Lady feigned ignorance and seemed like she might want to resist.

"Now stay there, and keep your fuckin' face down before I shoot it off," he told her, as a warning on the way out the door with the phone he'd taken from her now stuffed and stashed inside one side pocket of the pants he had on.

The two FBI agents looked at each other. It was too bad about the two men on the security team who had both been shot and killed. And to them, the money the robbers got away with didn't matter much either; it was all insured. Their main purpose of following the First Lady there to the bank that morning was to get the phone from her when she came back out.

"Don't worry, the video's hidden," said the First Lady. "I put it in a special file that'll be hard for anybody to find. You'll really have to know what you're doing in order to find it."

Marks and Wheeler weren't convinced.

"It's a new iPhone, in a pink carrying case," the First Lady said when the two special agents started to walk away.

***

About a mile away, with the getaway van still making distance, a conversation was started between two of the now unmasked robbers.

"What was it you took off the old broad?" asked the one in charge.

"A phone...she was filming us."

"You shoulda' left it."

"Why? They might've been able to use it to identify us."

"What, you don't think the bank's cameras didn't get us all on film?"

"Yeah, but..."

"Yeah, but nothin'. Those things are traceable. Now get rid of it."

"Yeah, alright...calm down. The first chance I get, I'll get rid of it," the second robber said, not liking the idea of being told what to do, "or bein' talked to like a peon."

But later, he didn't get rid of the phone. He forgot all about it. Something that would later cost him his life and might cause the rest of the crew to be caught too.

Chapter 3

Back at the bank

The bank and the entire area around the bank had been cordoned off. Present were special agents from the FBI, officers of the Philadelphia PD, ATF agents, and high-ranking officers of the security company responsible for the safety of the governor and The First Lady. They were there mainly because two of their officers had been killed.

Other than the First Lady's bold fiasco, trying to get the heist on film, everybody else had followed orders, and nobody inside the bank was hurt. But outside, the two security officers were killed mercilessly and without hesitation, something that didn't sit too well with those in charge.

A heavy downpour now covered the area as well, adding another source of perplexity and distress. Tensions were high, to say the least. But regardless of how bad the weather was and how hard the rain was coming down, everybody there wanted answers, and the men responsible for the robbery/murder caught and put in jail.

***

Bank robberies usually fell under the jurisdiction of the Federal Bureau of Investigation, but in this particular incidence, the case was handed down to officers of the Philadelphia Police Department. The lead investigator was Investigator Tyler Murphy.

"Marks and Wheeler, how is it that the two of you happen to be here on the scene?" asked Murphy after finally getting around to questioning the two FBI agents.

He'd already talked to other witnesses and had been told and updated about everything else known about the robbery. The two special agents had been told to wait and happened to be last on Murphy's list of people he wanted to question and get information from, something that didn't sit too well with either of them.

It just so happened that Special Agents Marks and Wheeler were both suspected of being corrupt and dishonest, and neither held much trust or respect. Nothing had been proven, but several complaints had been made stating that in the past, Marks and Wheeler had robbed drug dealers of their money and drugs instead of making an arrest and legally confiscating the drugs and money to be used as evidence.

They'd also been accused of brutality and even murder. Therefore, what either of the two special agents had to say wouldn't be valued very much as credible information anyway.

Special Agent Marks had his phone out and was on a call. So, Wheeler was the one responding to Murphy.

"We were here, escorting the First Lady," said Wheeler, not liking the idea of being questioned, especially not in the suspicious, distrustful tone of voice in which the question was asked. Wheeler, at six feet one, two hundred and thirty pounds, was built like a tank and wasn't easily intimidated and wouldn't be, not by Murphy, a Robert De Niro look-alike who was shorter and about thirty pounds lighter.

"Uh-huh," said Investigator Murphy, not bothering to hide the sarcasm or his feelings of distrust and of being suspicious of the two FBI agents.

"And is this now what, a new special practice of the FBI, to serve as an escort while the First Lady runs bank errands?"

"You know what, Murphy? Fuck you. I don't have to answer your damn questions. This is supposed to be a federal case anyway."

"I don't know about that, not according to my boss it isn't, nor yours. And with two dead and a million point three in cash missing from the bank? I'd say you'd have to answer to any damn thing I say you have to answer."

"Oh yeah? Okay...we'll see about that," said Special Agent Wheeler, turning to walk away. Heading towards the car, he said, "Let's go," to Special Agent Marks, who'd gotten off the phone and had, for the most part, been listening and looking on. Marks was a muscular, six foot-six, cornbread-fed white guy from Iowa who could kill without showing so much as an inkling of emotions; he wouldn't be easily intimidated either.

"Hey, where the hell do you two think you're goin'? I'm not finished," said Murphy, clearly bothered by the two Special

Agents' disregard for him and his authority.

"Where are we goin'?" asked Special Agent Wheeler, turning to share an inappropriate smile with the investigator. "Somewhere far from you, you can be sure of that," he said after he'd gotten in, slamming the car door shut. Marks got in, and the door on the other side of the car slammed shut immediately afterward.

"Asshole," thought Wheeler, starting and putting the car in gear. A moment later, he had the car and, with them in it speeding away.

Inside the car, Special Agent Marks's phone rang again.

"Hello."

"What the hell happened?" the husky voice on the other end asked. It was the governor, Governor Dillon Olamay.

A governor tough on crime, a governor for the people! was his slogan.

It was his second term as governor. Nevertheless, rumor had it that Governor Olamay was a homosexual, only pretending to be heterosexual. And that his marriage to Elaine Olamay was only a front to appease the tough Republicans who faithfully voted for him. What Elaine got out of being married to him was money and lots of it.

"The bank got robbed, and one of the robbers took the First Lady's phone," Marks told the governor.

"Damn, it!!! I bet the bitch was trying to record them."

"We gotta get that phone back. What are you two doin' about it?"

"We're just leavin' the scene. But don't worry; cell phones have tracking devices. We'll find it."

"You better, or all our ass'll be in a sling."

"Don't worry, we'll find it."

"Okay, keep me posted."

"Will do," said Special Agent Marks. But by then, the governor had already hung up.

"Let me guess, he's insisting we find the phone," said Wheeler.

"Yeah, somethin' like that."

"Yeah, well, if it wasn't for him, we wouldn't be in this damn mess."

"Tell me about it," said Special Agent Marks, drifting off in thought, starting to worry, actually.

The rest of the ride went by in silence. The two were on their way to see a friend, Harry Burgess, a redhead kid from South Carolina. An unstylish, unattractive guy who only showed interest in technical objects like computers and so forth, and hence a nerd. Harry worked for the FBI as well, but, of course, as a technician. He'd never actually worked in the field, had supposedly never fired a gun other than at a gun range, and definitely wasn't supposed to have ever killed anybody.

He actually hates violence and can always be found in the lab, working on some new gizmo or another, the rest of the agents would say.

His specialty, though, is trackin' phones or any other kind of technical device, like James Bond's Q of the 007 movies.

Chapter 4

Jake Winston was the bank robber who'd taken the First Lady's phone away from her. Most people who knew Jake were afraid of him, and for a good reason. He was way too cocky and dangerous and much too big to be questioned about it at six foot three, two hundred and forty pounds, much too unpredictable to even be trusted.

Macho Jake Winston was what his friends from high school called him, a rather mild description of his actual personality since high school.

Now considered *the stud of studs...a man's man,* a man who'd grown to be huge in size and attitude and had, in most instances, become aggressively virile to the point of being rude and obnoxious. But he loved Angel Clark, aka Heaven Neveah.

They met at the bar of a strip club, one of the few nights when Jake didn't get himself into some kind of fight or altercation.

Besides being the asshole that most people thought he was,

Jake also happened to be a very handsome guy. Nevertheless, it was Jake's bad boy bravado that turned Angel on the most, that and his willingness to throw caution to the wind.

"Besides a guy bein' handsome, if he isn't rough and rowdy, then what's the use?" she thought, considering the kind of men she always seemed to fall for and like.

Later that night, after meeting, talking, and drinking, he and Angel went home together and have been together ever since.

"A little over six months," she thought, reminiscing back to when the two first met.

Well, after the robbery, Angel was waiting in Jake's second-floor rowhouse apartment when Jake got home.

"What did you bring me?" she asked, smiling at Jake when he came walking through the door.

"This," he said proudly, taking the backpack off that he had on, emptying the contents of it on Angel and the bed she was on. $200,000, his take of the money from the bank robbery. It probably wasn't a smart thing to do, bringing the money from a bank robbery home with him. None of the other guys did it; they had all stashed their share of the money in separate, secure locations. But not Jake. His arrogance and stupidity wouldn't let him be afraid or even cautious. Besides, he wanted to show off and impress Angel, which was why she waited there in his apartment. He asked her to wait and promised a surprise when he got home.

"You're an animal," she said, later to flatter Jake and boost his ego while he made love to her. The compliment seemed only to ignite a flame and fuel Jake's energy and passion. It sent Jake's sex drive into overdrive, making him go harder, deeper, and faster.

And in just minutes, the two were gasping for air and panting from reaching the highest point during the sexual explosion Jake had set off.

Later, line after line of meth and coke kept them wired for sound and up all night. They drank Bud Light and Jack Daniels and smoked marijuana to mellow out. But still, being high on meth wouldn't let them sleep.

Sex was something neither of them seemed not to ever get enough of, but after so many times, even that got old. Jake eventually busied himself cleaning his precious Glock seventeen, his favorite toy and protector, a gun that he loved and cherished, probably more, or at least as much as he did Angel. He never left the house without it, that's for sure.

Angel busied herself cleaning the house. And everything was fine until she started to do laundry and found Jake's pants, the same pants he'd worn during the robbery.

The First Lady's phone was still in it, the same phone he was told to get rid of.

"Who does this belong to?" Angel asked, holding it up so Jake could see it. The phone was the newest version of the iPhone, very high-tech and expensive.

The case was pink, obviously not a color for a phone fitting Jake's everlasting hard-core demeanor and character.

"No, this phone belongs to a woman," thought Angel, becoming more and more hurt and unglued by the minute.

Jake was at a loss for words, realizing the mistake he'd made. He remembered being told, "Those things are traceable. Now get rid of it."

"Is she pretty?" Angel asked when Jake still hadn't said anything. The question brought him out of the thought he was having.

"What? Oh, no. I took that off a broad during the robbery. I forgot it was still in my pants pocket."

"Shit!!!" he thought.

Angel didn't believe him. A handsome guy like Jake, women were always throwing themselves at him.

"You don't have to lie, Jake. Please, just tell the truth."

"Do you love her?" Angel asked, not knowing what else to say, clearly heartbroken. Tears had formed and were now starting to fall in constant streams.

"Awww, babe, no, it's not like that at all. And I am tellin' you the truth, I promise."

"On the way out the bank, I caught an old broad tryin' to record us. So, I took the phone from her. I was actually supposed to have gotten rid of it, but I forgot I even had it."

"Come on, babe, I swear. I love you, not nobody else."

Luckily for Jake, Angel turned on the phone and found it still accessible. And sure enough, footage of them robbing the bank was still on it.

Angel smiled and turned the screen so he could see it.

"See, I told you," said Jake, relieved that the story he told her was proven.

"Sorry, babe," said Angel, still smiling while wiping the tears away. Curiosity made her inspect the phone further.

"These aren't even out yet," thought Angel, which was true; the First Lady had ordered the phone and had it made just for her. It was new, one-of-a-kind. The First Lady hadn't even put a security code in or made a call on it and had only used it to make a recording in the bank and a recording of something else in one other instance.

The whole time, Angel hadn't stopped pressing buttons and swiping the screen. Seeing how taken she was with it made Jake throw even more caution to the wind and ask, "You like it?"

The question made Angel look up at him immediately, but only momentarily to smile again and give him a nod.

"If you like it so much, keep it then," Jake told her, which was like rewarding a kid with a new favorite toy at Christmas. Just the day before, Angel had dropped her phone and shattered the screen, needing a new phone anyway. Later, she would load all of her contacts, pictures, and Facebook information on the pink phone and would become seriously attached to it.

"Awwww, babe...thank you," she said, rewarding Jake too with another smile, and this time a big hug and a kiss.

"You're the best," she said afterward; before the two started with even more kisses. A moment or two later, Jake had Angel back on the bed, banging away inside of her again.

***

The two FBI special agents didn't go to sleep that night either, and neither did Harry Burgess. The two agents were at a diner having breakfast and coffee when Special Agent Marks's phone rang. Harry Burgess' name popped up on the screen.

"Harry! What you got for me?" asked Special Agent Marks.

"The First Lady's phone, I got a hit on it. It hasn't moved all night. You want the address?"

"Yeah, wait..." said Marks, switching hands to hold the phone, so excited he almost dropped it. At the same time, digging in the inside pocket of the suit jacket he had on, looking for a pen and paper.

"Alright...the address...give it to me," he said after coming out with the pen and paper that he needed.

***

After more than an hour of constantly making love, Jake, all sweaty and out of breath, finally rolled over, exhausted. He'd just gotten up to go to the bathroom when somebody started banging on the door. But only the police would bang on a door like this person was banging, extremely hard, and in successions... *like they were out of their mind, trying to bang the damn thing off the hinges.*

Jake immediately grabbed the Glock Seventeen and jacked a round in the chamber.

"Who The Fuck Is It!?!" he yelled and asked, unafraid and ready to confront whoever the bastards were, police or not; Jake didn't give a damn. They must not have known, for they were banging on the door of Jake Winston's house.

He only made it halfway to the door, though, proceeding with heavy footsteps, before the blast from a 12-gauge shotgun came through and killed Jake. He lay there on the floor, naked, still holding the gun, but with a big hole in him where his stomach used to be.

Jake never bothered to buy much furniture, so it only took Angel to peep around the bedroom door into the living room to know what was happening. There was Jake, all sprawled out on the floor in a pool of his own blood. Common sense told her that whoever shot through the door and killed him would eventually come through the door and kill her too. They were already kicking it...one kick, two kicks...

There was no time to waste crying or worrying about Jake. He was dead, and the same fate would come to her if she didn't hurry. She put on the jeans that she'd been wearing the day before but only had time to grab the shirt and shoes and carry them...oh, and the phone. She'd left it there on top of the jeans she'd just put on.

In less than ten seconds, she was out the window and making her way quickly down the second-floor fire escape. She was only able to run so far down the alley, though, before having to stop to put on the shoes and shirt. The shoes, especially after how much glass and other debris she'd stepped on. That's when she looked back and into the eyes of Special Agent Wheeler, the man she presumed had just shot Jake. He was halfway out the window, about to come after her.

Chapter 5

"Harry, we're at the address you gave us, but we can't find the phone."

"That's because it's not there anymore. I guess when you guys arrived, whoever had it took off with it." Marks then told Burgess about the girl Wheeler saw running down the alley.

"There's an army surplus store not far from you, on the corner of Wabash and Crane. That's where the phone is now. You might find her there too," said Burgess.

"You know the place I'm talkin' about?"

"Yeah, I know exactly where it is. We're headed there now. Keep me informed, and let us know if it moves again."

"Will do," said Harry, his eyes now glued to the locator, monitoring the phone's movement.

Next, Marks put in a call to Murphy to inform him of their location and that they'd found some of the bank's money from the robbery. The thought was that this would get them in good with Murphy. However, it was never mentioned that both men had taken a bundle of hundred-dollar bills from the bank money for themselves, $20,000 each.

"It won't be missed. And if it is, they'll only think somebody else got it, not us," the two officers were thinking.

On the way out the door, Wheeler, noticing Jake's hand still holding the Glock Seventeen, said, "Wait, let's cover our asses."

With that, he had Marks look out to make sure nobody was out in the hallway. And then, after Marks closed the door, Wheeler picked up Jake's hand holding the gun and fired a shot through the door.

"Now we can say that he fired at us first," Wheeler said, and Marks agreed.

***

The city was plagued by rain again, and the temperature in the mid-forties felt quite cool for an early September autumn day.

Angel had no idea why Jake had been killed or why she'd been forced to run. All she knew was that dying the way Jake had died wasn't the way she wanted to go. So, if running meant living, then run she must.

The first store she came to was an old army surplus store on the corner of Wabash, and Crane Street, about a mile or so away from where Jake lived. If for no other reason, she went inside to get out of the rain. But once inside, she saw an old army jacket she wanted to buy and a hat. The jacket turned out to be quite warm and comfortable.

"...and a great disguise," she thought, looking at herself in the mirror. And then she saw an old army bag; small but neat, and it had a strap that she could throw over a shoulder. It looked like a purse, whether it was one or not, and it matched the coat and hat perfectly.

Then she thought about all the money Jake had come home with and how now she needed it. But there'd been no time, no time to grab not a single dollar. The only money she had now was a measly hundred-dollar bill left over from the check she received every month.

"How much?" she asked the young, black male clerk who seemed mesmerized by her; not only was she pretty, but the jeans Angel had on fit like a glove, exposing the kind of curves the kid had never seen before, at least not up close and in person.

"I don't know, let's find out," he said, coming closer to get a look at the price tags on all the items and a closer look at Angel.

"A hundred thirty-five plus tax," he said afterward, after surveying the price tags and getting an eye full of Angel's sexy body.

Angel had the hundred-dollar bill in her hand, held up so he could see it.

"We'll use my discount and call it a hundred even," the kid said, sharing a wink and a smile. The kid, at twenty years old, owned the store, something that had been in the family since World War II. His grandfather, a veteran of the war, owned it, and then his dad, and now he owned it. The store was passed down after his father passed away; a terrible bout with prostate cancer killed him.

Next, Angel asked, "Is there a bathroom?"

"Yeah, back there," the kid said before a car outside came to a screeching halt in front of the store.

Angel had made it almost to where the kid pointed when she looked back and saw the same guy get out of the car that she'd seen coming out the window at Jake's house. There was another guy with him. The two guys looked like cops, but how could she be sure? Or better yet, how could she trust them? Jake had just been killed by these guys, and now, for some reason, they were coming after her.

The kid saw the two bulky guys and took them to be some sort of law enforcement officers as well. But he also saw the fearful, worried look on Angel's face and, early on, made a decision about whose side he would be on.

"Is there anybody else here with you?" Marks asked, coming through the front door, gun in hand.

"No," the kid said, nervous as hell, and who now needed to use the bathroom too.

"Don't lie," Wheeler said to intimidate the kid.

"I'm not," the kid answered, gaining confidence. He'd seen cop shows like *The First 48,* in which the police always use the same scare tactics. It was always the weakling who broke down and told everything the cops wanted to know, information which, in most cases, was then used in court against the same person who told them.

Well, it wouldn't be him as the weakling, not with the life of one of the sexiest women he'd ever seen at stake, not in his store.

"'Captain-save-a-hoe' it is, then," he thought, sticking by the

decision he'd made and gaining even more confidence by the minute.

Angel had run past the bathroom in the back and had hidden behind boxes stacked high in a dark storage room. The room was infested with rats, and Angel almost screamed when one ran across her foot.

While Special Agent Marks talked to and questioned the kid, Special Agent Wheeler busied himself inspecting the rest of the store. He had a gun in hand and had ventured into the back room as well. First, he opened the bathroom door, found it empty, and was just about to go into the dark storage area where Angel had hidden. But then, several rats, startled by Angel's presence, ran out and stunned the hell out of Wheeler.

"Damn, it!!! I hate rats," he cursed, turning back towards the front of the store. When he got there, Marks was busy interrogating the kid.

"We're lookin' for a girl, white, about 5'7" tall, long hair, fine as hell. Have you seen her?"

Like the bank, the surplus store had two doors, too, on two adjacent streets. The kid didn't give a direct answer to Marks's question, but he did advert his eyes and head towards the second door.

"Thank you," said Marks, in a hurry to get out and see if maybe he could catch a glimpse of Angel running or walking down the sidewalk.

Angel didn't know it, but the bag she'd just bought wasn't just an ordinary bag to carry things in. It happened to be an *Off Grid Faraday* bag, a bag used by law enforcement and by those in the intelligence division of the military.

The bag was first used in World War II by spies on both sides of the Berlin Wall. Although the bag looked normal, the same color as all the other olive-green pieces of uniform soldiers of the army wore, it was actually lined with lead and used to transport secret electronic devices. Once the devices were placed inside of it, they immediately became undetectable by tracking devices. Luckily Angel had placed the phone inside of it, and when Marks called to ask Harry Burgess for an update, the answer he got was, "Nothing, I lost the signal."

Angel waited a while before she came out, not until the kid told her the coast was clear and that the two law enforcement officers were gone. By then, both the kid and Angel were in desperate need of using the bathroom.

It wouldn't be until an hour later that Angel would use the phone again, this time to call Giovanni to ask for money. She felt she needed to get away for a while.

"Miami," she thought. She had a friend there who assured her a girl like her would get rich.

"Girl, millionaires are in the club all the time, dyin' to meet a pretty lil' thing like you."

Lately, Giovanni had gotten stingy with all his money, which was why she only asked him for enough money to buy a train ticket, not a plane ticket. Instead, he was sending a guy named Trent Walker to get her.

She'd heard about Trent, a top-notch record producer, but they'd never actually met.

"Whatever," she thought, *"As long as he hurries and doesn't try to get fresh on our way to Miami, I'm really not in the mood."*

When she hung up, she put the phone right back in the bag and then walked twenty blocks or so to a friend's house. She would be safe until Trent got there.

***

Back at Jake's apartment, the whole unit of Philadelphia PD had arrived, with the forensics team checking and going over everything. When Marks and Wheeler walked in, Inspector Murphy was on the floor, checking Jake's body.

"Jesus...did you guys have to shoot through the door and kill him?" he asked, talking to both special agents.

It was Wheeler who answered.

"Yeah...he shot first, we shot back." Murphy had doubts that it was not what actually happened but was unwilling to argue, especially since they'd called and told him about the money.

"How did you find out about the place?" asked Murphy, again, a question asked for both special agents.

This time it was Marks who answered.

"We got a tip from one of our CIs."

"You mind tellin' me who the CI is?" Murphy asked.

"Not a chance," Marks responded, which ended the questions.

"There was a girl here with him," said Marks about Jake. "She climbed out the window and ran down the alley. Let us know if you get a hit on prints. We need to find her, and fast," said Wheeler.

"What, you think she might've had somethin' to do with the robbery?" asked Murphy.

"We're not sure. But according to our CI, she could be involved in another case we're investigating. So, we would appreciate it if you let us know what you find."

"Okay, as you can see, the forensics team is already checkin' for prints now. I'll let you know if we find something."

And with that, both Marks and Wheeler left the room. Harry Burgess told them about the brief blip on the locator screen, but the phone's tracking device wasn't on long enough to get an exact location.

"The girl's smart, whoever she is. Army surplus stores sometimes sell bags that block the signal of tracking devices. They're called *Off Grid Faraday Bags.* I bet she bought one while she was there, which might explain why we lost the signal. If she is that smart, we've probably lost her for good."

"She's not that smart, Harry, believe me. If she did buy such a bag, it would've been by chance. As far as I know, she doesn't even know we're looking for the phone or why. So, keep trying to find it, okay?" said Marks, not liking what Harry had to say, something that was starting to make him worry more.

"Okay, I'll let you know when I find somethin' for sure," Harry told Marks before the two hung up the phone.

Marks relayed to Wheeler what Burgess said.

"You think she might've looked in the phone and saw the video of us?" Wheeler asked, worried now as well.

"I doubt it; we'd be in jail if she had."

"The boyfriend probably just gave her the phone as a gift, not knowing anything else about it. And now, after seeing him killed, she more than likely panicked and took the phone with her."

"And remember, it was cold and raining. So, I'm willing to bet she bought more than just a bag from the army surplus store."

After a brief stop back at the army surplus store, the kid confirmed that Angel had indeed bought a bag, but she'd also bought a matching jacket and hat, a complete outfit, which confirmed Marks's prediction, and brought some sort of relief to both special agents.

It wouldn't be until the next day when Burgess called again, giving them a new location of the phone, but until then, the two special agents would nonetheless still lose sleep worrying about it.

Chapter 6

A premonition was what made my mother decide that when I was born, I would be called Trent, Trent Walker. The original Trent Walker had been an uncle of hers who died a hero in Vietnam during the war.

The premonition told her that I would one day become a hero as well. I took it as a warning, though, when she told me about it, a warning that one day I, too, would die unnecessarily trying to save the life of somebody who really wasn't worth it.

The same thought came back to me the day I met Angel Clark. Somehow I knew that she would be trouble and that the burden of it would fall on me.

"Gee. Thanks, Giorgio, my good friend."

I thought this even before ever being shot or hit in the head, causing me to suffer from an acute form of amnesia. And before then, I swore I would never get involved with her. That was before she and I had ever met.

"Hey, turn that thing down," she said about the radio. "Oh, and on the way, I need for you to stop in Richmond and in St. Augustine, just south of Jacksonville," she said after only being on the passenger side of the SUV for thirty seconds.

"Already givin' me orders," I thought, without actually saying it.

I asked her, "Do you mind if we at least get on the road first before you start tellin' me what to do, suggesting where we need to stop?" I was tempted to offer her the keys and ask if she wanted to drive. I thought differently of it, thinking she might take me up on the offer.

Anyway, what I said made her smile. From being so beautiful, she was obviously used to getting her way. It had become a habit, telling people what to do, men especially, whom I was sure were like putty in Angel's hands.

And to have a guy finally stand up to her was a turn-on, especially since she liked and found me attractive, something she told me later on in a conversation.

I wasn't the next Denzel Washington or Idris Elba, but I did consider myself attractive in the sense of being well-built from working out and from always being well-groomed and mannerable, which I thought was most important.

My stepmother always told me that being respectable and having good manners would take me a long way in life. And that *if you treat a woman right, she'll always be good to you.*

"But don't be nobody's fool either, Trent. Weakness is somethin' that's not attractive," she told me. The woman my father left my mother for turned out to be very smart and a damn good teacher, somebody I ended up learning very valuable lessons from.

The smile Angel shared was from admiration. It was still early on, but so far, she couldn't help but like and approve of the way I handled and carried myself.

"Sorry," she said, for how she'd gotten in the car, rudely giving me orders on what to do. Instead, now reconsidering how to deal with me. I'd become a challenge already.

It wouldn't be until an hour later before she smiled and said anything else, but when she did speak, it was with kindness and respect.

"I have to use the bathroom. Can we stop somewhere, please?"

"Yeah, sure," I said, noticing and liking the change. We'd just passed Baltimore and were nearing DC. I could use a bathroom break too.

***

Marks and Wheeler had both finally decided to go home and rest for a while, but before Marks could close his eyes, the phone rang. It was Harry Burgess.

"The girl and the phone, they're traveling south on I-76. They're at a gas station, the Maryland House Rest Area, past Baltimore, near DC."

After hanging up the phone with Harry, the phone rang again,

"Marks." It was Tyler Murphy. He continued, "We got a hit on two sets of prints in the dead guy's apartment. One set belongs to him. He's Jake Winston. The other set of prints belongs to an Angel

Clark, from the Jacksonville, Florida area, St. Augustine."

"Which is where she's probably headed to now," thought Marks, remembering what Harry had told him about the phone and the girl moving south on I-76, which would run them into I-95 south, the interstate to take if you wanted to go south, to Florida.

"I got a file on her if you want to come to copy it, pictures included," Murphy said to finish what he had to say.

"I'm on my way," said Marks, forcing himself out of bed.

Next, he called Wheeler.

"Get up. I'm on my way to come get you. Oh, and pack a few clothes and things. We're headed to Florida."

"Shit," said Wheeler, forcing himself out of bed too. "I was just startin' to doze off."

"Alright... I'll be ready when you get here."

Chapter 7

There was a line of folks waiting to use both the men's and ladies' restrooms, so it took a while to actually get in to relieve ourselves. Afterward, I thought about topping off the gas tank but thought against it after seeing that there was a long line at all the pumps to get gas too.

Angel was in the SUV; she had the phone out and was on the web page, browsing through Facebook like she'd been doing beforehand, before we got there, something that seemed to have captured her full attention. I was about to ask if she might be hungry and wanted something to eat, but then I remembered the three thousand dollars Giorgio had sent.

"I almost forgot," I said, handing it to her.

"What's this?" she asked, surprised but taking it.

"Giorgio."

"Oh, he sent it anyway, huh?" she said, smiling at me. The smile seemed genuine, catching me off guard, and for a moment, my heart seemed to skip a beat.

"No! Don't even think about it," I told myself about the feeling I thought I might already be starting to have about liking Angel. But how could I not like her? She was beautiful. If inside of her was a personality anywhere near as beautiful as Angel was, who I saw smiling at me, then it was a wrap. Falling in love would be next, something more likely to happen than the sun rising every morning.

"Are you hungry or anything?" I asked anyway, just so I could look at her again.

"No, I'm fine," she said, smiling again. And there it was again, another instance when it felt like my heart might've skipped a beat.

"Okay, I guess we'll get goin' then," I said, just for the hell of it. A smile was now on my face too, and suddenly I felt good about meeting and having her in the SUV, sitting beside me.

"Why are you smiling?" she asked, looking over at me, not in a way as if the smile on my face bothered her, but asking innocently, in a way that showed genuine interest. And then, even the way she spoke was starting to get to me.

"Oh, nothin'. Just a thought," I said in response, starting the SUV, anxious to get us back on the road again.

That's when Angel put the phone back in the bag, that and the money I'd just given her.

"You mind sharing?"

"What, the thought I was just havin'?"

"Yeah. It was about me, wasn't it?"

"That obvious, huh?" I said, smiling again. Angel laughed. It was getting more and more obvious that I was starting to like her.

"Okay, forget the thought," she said, turning towards me, looking as gorgeous as ever. "Tell me about yourself, Trent Walker, and how you became to be such a successful writer and record producer. Yeah, I've heard about you, all the hit songs you've written, and famous artists you've produced for."

"What'a you wanna know?" I asked, surprised that not only she'd heard of me but that now she was also interested to know more about who I might be.

"Everything. Start from the beginning. You know, like, 'I was born in...' from that beginning."

"What? About me?" I asked, now feeling a bit embarrassed about suddenly being in the spotlight. I wrote and produced songs for other people to perform live onstage, but being in the spotlight was personally something that bothered me. It definitely wasn't my forte.

But then, something had come over me, a rather strange sensation. Seeing the look in Angel's eyes made me want to do all I could to please her. I remembered Giorgio saying, "Never fall in love with a stripper." Thinking about it brought another smile to my face because that's exactly what I was starting to do, fall in love with a stripper.

While driving, the next thing I knew, I was spilling my guts, telling Angel everything, the whole story about my life.

"I was born in Albany, Georgia," I said, looking over, smiling at her, "but grew up in Detroit and New York. My mother lived in Detroit. Dad lived on Long Island, New York. I used to go back and forth between the two; a year here, a summer there.

"After graduating high school, I joined the Navy and got *Brother Duty* with Greg, a brother of mine whom I'd only met once before. He and I were only a month apart, virtually the same age. I was born in October, and Greg was born in November.

"Turns out, before leaving Albany to move to New York, Dad had gotten two women pregnant at the same time; my mother and Greg's mother. Moving to New York was his escape. Greg and I had two other younger brothers, but they both lived there on Long Island with Dad and his wife, their mother.

"Anyway, after joining the Navy, I went back to Detroit to marry my high school sweetheart. We weren't really in love, but we had a son together already. I was determined to bring my son up having both his mother and father, so I married her to ensure that my son would indeed have both of us. Big mistake on my part.

"After only two years of bein' in the Navy, she and I separated. The separation would lead to a very unhappy divorce. Unhappy because I'd fallen in love with her after all and was heartbroken when she left, and we'd called it quits officially.

"There were quite a few other bad decisions I'd made afterward, including departing from the Navy, which ended in a bad conduct discharge.

"I moved to Florida after that… Orlando. It wasn't what I'd planned to do, but during a visit to Mom and the new husband she'd married, I got a job at Disney and decided to stay. I eventually became a flight attendant, and during one particular flight, I met Giorgio, who I ran into on several other flights as well. After hearing a song I'd written, it was he who convinced me that I had talent as a writer/record producer. I eventually made the move to New York, and the rest is history.

"Quite a boring story, huh?"

"No, not at all," said Angel, who seemed mesmerized by what I'd just told her.

"I'm sure you left a lot out, but okay, Trent Walker," she seemed actually impressed.

Although quite handsome and attractive, Trent still wasn't Angel's type.

"Doesn't mean we can't be friends, though," she thought, warming to the idea.

A solemn look then came on Angel's face. It was her turn to talk and talk about who she was.

Turns out, Angel was a military brat. Her father had been in the Navy as well, stationed onboard an aircraft carrier at the Mayport Naval Station in Jacksonville. He'd suffered somewhat of the same fate that I'd suffered; marriage, separation, bad divorce, and kids left without a stable family.

"One of Dad's friends even raped me. But Dad shot him and was sentenced to five years for manslaughter. That would be the last time my sister and I would ever see him alive. He was stabbed and killed during a fight in prison. Mom eventually became a doctor but died five years later from Lupus. She came here from Ireland as an exchange student to study and attend classes at Mercer University in Macon, Georgia. She met and married Dad during spring break in Florida one year and never went back to Ireland.

"After the divorce, she went back to Mercer and graduated at the top of her class. It's too bad that after it was all said and done, helping and saving people, she was unable to help or save herself.

"I miss her so much," said Angel, suddenly fighting back tears. I could see that it was hard for her to tell this part of the story.

"My sister, Adele, is who I wanna stop to see in Richmond. It's been a little over a year since I've heard from or seen her. We're twins, and basically, each other is all we have. Uncle Johnny, my father's brother, and his wife have a house on the beach in St. Augustine, but other than them and their two sons, we have no other family.

"So, that's why I got in the car asking you to stop in those places. Sorry if the way I asked came out wrong. It's just that my life is a mess right now, and I'd really like to see them, maybe for the last time," Angel said, no longer able to hold in tears from pain that had been disguised and hidden for so long.

Just then, a few miles after we had gone past the Washington DC area and had crossed into Virginia, a sign on the side of the road said, *Richmond 78 miles,* which I had already determined would be our very next stop.

Chapter 8

Adele Clark/Madison

With Angel Clark's stage name being *Heaven Neveah*, something pleasant or good, Adele's stage name, if she had been a stripper, would've been *The Witch*, not because she was a devil worshipper, or even portrayed herself as one, but people thought that of her simply because she was different.

Different, however, in ways nobody understood, maybe as if she were a predictor, or a prophet, not like the prophets known of the Christianity religion or of Islam, but a prophet nonetheless.

Adele was pretty, very pretty, actually, and had an exceptionally nice body just like Angel's, but right away, I could tell the two were actually nothing alike, more like night and day.

When we got there, she ran out, opened Angel's door, and helped her out. The two sisters then hugged and embraced each other and carried on as if they really did miss each other. But when she came over to me, she grabbed my hand and wouldn't let go.

"Hi, you're Giorgio's friend, right?" she asked.

"I am," I said, wondering how she knew.

"Trent Walker."

"Adele Madison," she said, still with a firm grip, holding onto my hand. The whole time she was smirking and had a look in her eyes as if she could see straight through me, down to what color underwear I had on, as well as comprehending my every thought. And when she spoke, it was in a tone of voice that sounded eerie and hypnotizing. I was definitely dazzled and overcome by it.

The house Adele lived in was actually on the outskirts of Richmond, just outside city limits, in what turned out to be a farmhouse, complete with a barn, stables, and lots of animals, dogs and cats mostly.

She'd married early, fresh out of high school. However, supposedly her husband, Bill Madison, had recently committed suicide by locking himself inside the barn with an old tractor that he'd left running. After drinking a whole fifth of Wild Turkey, he supposedly passed out and died a slow death from Carbon Monoxide poisoning.

The house then belonged solely to Adele. It had five bedrooms, four of which Adele rented out, to drug addicts and the homeless as far as I could tell. Two were on the roof making repairs when Angel and I got there, which I imagined was how the two paid their share for room and board, doing odd jobs in and around the house and property.

"They definitely didn't look like they might've had any money whether they did or not."

After a while, Angel finally had to come over and literally separate Adele's hand from mine.

"She wouldn't let go."

Adele just laughed.

"Come on, let's go inside. And please, bring your friend," she told Angel while leading the way inside the house but looking back at me too. Neither of us said it, but Angel thought Adele had lost her mind, and so did I.

On the way in, I noticed a rather large Oak tree on the far-left side of Adele's yard.

I'd never seen an Oak this large.

Under it was a podium made of stone, and twelve seats in front of it, also made of stone. In all, a place for thirteen individuals to meet and assemble. The mystic of the number thirteen was what got me, thirteen being the number I recognized as a symbol of bad luck and misfortune.

Nothing darker and more malevolent than Friday the 13th.

The whole setup was weird as hell.

Later, from one of the workers, I would learn that strange people would come and take seats in front of the podium, people who had emerged from out of the woods or from the overgrown fields.

People who were old and frail. However, none of these people would ever arrive by car or truck.

Or by any other real normal means of transportation.

The boarders and workers themselves weren't allowed at the meetings, nor did Adele even want them close. *Or over in that particular area at all.*

"She would yell, scream and curse if she did see or suspect that we'd violated the area around the podium," one worker told me.

Once inside the house, right away, I started noticing things, items around the house; a crystal ball, a whole collection of oils that had been put in different bottles, a collection of small bones as well, and tarot cards,

Some off the deck and turned over already.

Even more startling was a picture on the wall above the fireplace mantel. The painting was somewhat of an excellent portrait of a man's face. However, somehow it seemed that everywhere I went, the eyes on the picture moved and followed me. Adele laughed again after seeing the startled look on my face.

Angel didn't comment or know what to think and didn't bother even asking about it. But instead said, "Adele...come, so we can talk," taking Adele by the hand and leading her away.

"Excuse us, will you," Adele said, looking and smiling at me again.

Angel looked at me too.

"We'll be right back," she said before the two women disappeared into the next room.

I heard Adele say, "Girl, I like him! He's cute."

"Forget about Trent," said Angel, quickly changing the subject, "Where've you been? I called and called, but you never answered.

You had me worried about you."

"I'm alright," Adele said.

The conversation they were having turned a lot more private once the door to the back room was closed behind them.

In the meantime, I turned and headed back outside. The eyes on the portrait seemed to still be zoomed in on me, something that didn't make me feel too comfortable.

Outside, the two guys on the roof came down and started talking. I also noticed two other guys with rifles. They'd shot a deer and were dragging it out by the barn. Another guy was readying the barbecue grill. I'd never had deer meat before and really didn't want any now. But the idea of a barbecue was starting to make me hungry.

I was glad when Angel finally came out of the house.

"You ready?" she asked, knowing the answer already. She'd been in the house for more than twenty minutes. I'd taken up a spot, leaning back on the driver-side door of the SUV, a strong indication that, yes, I was ready to go, especially with twelve or so aggravating dogs and cats barking and sniffing around me.

Before we left, Angel insisted I take pictures of her and Adele, the two sisters, and she wanted me to take them with the new phone Jake had given her. She went on and on, bragging about it.

"It's the new iPhone, which has this and that, and a new, high-resolution lens, the best for taking pictures."

"Which'll take ten or fifteen more minutes," I thought and assumed, unimpressed with Angel's new iPhone. *Or about wasting more time trying to learn how to use it.*

***

Special Agent Marks not only stopped to pick up Special Agent Wheeler, but he also stopped and got Harry Burgess as well. Harry brought a laptop and the tracking device along. Therefore, the chances were slim and unlikely that the phone would ever get too far ahead or out of distance to be detected.

At the Maryland House rest area, nobody recognized the pictures that the special agents had of Angel or could actually say they remembered seeing her. But the surveillance cameras were a different story. Perfect pictures of Angel were captured, along with the SUV she was riding in and of me as the driver.

However, after leaving, and after Angel had put the phone back inside the bag so that she and I could talk, the FBI special agents had relatively been riding blindly, only assuming where we might be. All of that changed when Angel took the phone back out, insisting I take pictures.

"I got 'em," said Burgess, feeling triumphant. Over an hour had gone by since the last reading he'd gotten, and what he had now was an exact location, "They're at a farmhouse outside of Richmond."

Chapter 9

"Gentlemen. Can I help you?" Adele asked when the car stopped, and the two special agents got out.

"Yeah...FBI. And you can put your fuckin' hands up, NOW!!!" said Special Agent Wheeler, with his gun now drawn, aimed at Adele, whom he thought was Angel. Special Agent Marks pulled his gun and aimed it at her too.

It was then that two men came out of the barn; they had guns, assault rifles actually, aimed at the two special agents. Two men with rifles also came from behind the big Oak tree, and a man from each side of the house came out, all with guns aimed at the special agents.

"I'd put those down if I were you," Adele told Marks and Wheeler about the guns they had aimed at her. Before either special agent could move or respond, Adele turned and started walking towards the barn. But along the way, she turned again and told the two special agents.

"Come...follow me. Let's go inside. Let's talk," she told them, turning to walk towards the barn again.

By then, Special Agents Marks and Wheeler had both lowered and dropped their guns, and Harry Burgess had been forced out of the car too. It seemed they had no other choice than to follow Adele inside the barn. It was either that or take a chance on being shot right then and there by six men with assault rifles.

***

Once back on the interstate with the SUV cruising at eighty miles an hour, all was well again. Things were back on track as they should have been, with us traveling south towards the North Carolina, South Carolina, and Georgia state lines and then the Florida state line. After that, the next stop wouldn't be until we got to St. Augustine. Hopefully, the visit there wouldn't be very long either, no longer than the stop we'd made in Richmond.

Adele and Angel had obviously had a drink or two and smoked marijuana in the back room of the house before we left. Angel had dozed and fallen fast asleep, but the scent reeked, and the car smelled like both alcohol and marijuana. I wasn't bothered by it. She seemed relaxed. And with her asleep, I wouldn't have to worry about stopping so much, and we could cover some long miles getting us to where we wanted to go.

It still wasn't known what to expect in Miami, where to find Wild Boy Reed, or even where to start looking. The only thing Giorgio seemed to know about him was that Wild Boy Reed liked strip clubs. But a city like Miami had strip clubs everywhere, on every side of town, and more.

"How hard might it be to luck up and find the one Wild Boy

Reed might be in?"

"Very," I thought, with the scenario of finding a needle in a haystack in mind.

"Aww, worry about it later," I said, as a reminder that I hadn't even gotten there yet, and still had about ten hours or more to drive, not including the stop Angel wanted to make in St. Augustine.

The last time I'd been in the Jacksonville/St. Augustine area had been some years ago, quite a few, actually. Nevertheless, the thought of it still brought up bad feelings. Vicky, the love of my life back then, was who I took there.

We went there so that she could get an abortion, something that, in the end, broke both of our hearts.

"Never again," I thought to myself in the parking lot after the procedure was over and done, after I'd had time to think about and miss a child of mine who would never be born.

The worst day of my entire life, as it turned out to be.

We'd both made the decision to have it done, but afterward, we both sat in the parking lot and cried about it. I was still playing the field and didn't think I wanted to be tied down with the responsibilities that came with having a baby. Her reasons for wanting an abortion were that she'd already had one child out of wedlock and didn't want to have another under the same unmarried status.

Family members and the people at the church she went to would've frowned at it and thought terribly of her.

I did love Vicky and had very much considered asking her to marry me.

"Just not yet," I told myself, thinking she might be there, waiting for me forever. *The second big mistake I made with her.*

Since I wasn't ready to get married, she married another guy and did have his baby. And there I was, heartbroken again. From that day forward, I swore I would never love again, regardless of who might've been right or wrong for the decision Vicky and I had made. But then there I was in the car, looking over at Angel ever so often as if she were some sort of a goddess, the Goddess of Love, maybe, brought here on earth just to satisfy me.

"Maybe that's why Adele and Angel didn't ask if I wanted a drink or some of the weed they were smoking...I'm already high," I thought, feeling foolish for the way that I felt.

"She's no good," I heard myself say in my head about Angel, saying it over and over again, *"She's no good, she's no good."* But there I was, concentrating more on her than the road I was on, now hoping she would wake up and talk some more.

Thirty minutes later, she was awake and wanted to get off at the next exit. She was hungry and had to use the bathroom again.

***

"You gentlemen mind telling' me why you're here, on my property, pointing loaded guns at me?" Adele asked once she and the three unarmed FBI special agents and two of her men, both with rifles, were all inside the barn. The rest of the men who worked for Adele waited and kept watch outside.

"And do you have a warrant?" she asked, a question pertaining to the law. Not that it mattered; for the moment, there was no mistaking who was the one in charge.

"We don't need a warrant," Wheeler answered, the gutsier of the three special agents, with still no idea who Adele was.

"You have somethin' that doesn't belong to you, and we're here to get it back."

"Oh yeah? And what might that be?" Adele asked.

"The phone your boyfriend took from the governor's wife when he and his friends robbed the Bank of Philadelphia yesterday mornin'.

"If you'll just hand it over, we'll be on our way."

Adele laughed.

"Honey, I'm afraid you're mistaken on both accounts. First, I don't have a boyfriend who robs banks. And second...you're not goin' anywhere until I say you can go."

"Now cool your horses. I'll be back in a minute," she said, more to the armed men watching over the special agents, to keep them on guard.

A moment later, she was gone, on her way back inside the house to make a few phone calls. Adele's phone, however, was in one of her pants' back pockets as she turned to go. She pulled it out and made sure Wheeler could see it before leaving the room. It wasn't the one they were looking for, but Adele had a good idea who did have it.

***

At a McDonald's, only fifty or so miles south of Richmond, Angel and I sat at a table famished, eating Big Macs and fries. Adele was calling to warn us about the FBI, but we never heard the phone ring. Angel had left it and the bag in the Back seat of the SUV.

Chapter 10

Adele happened to know the sheriff of Chesterfield County, Virginia, personally; the two were good friends. After getting no answer on Angel's phone, a call to Sheriff Marty Stinson was the next call she made.

"You did what!?!" he asked when Adele told him about the three men she'd encountered at gunpoint who were now being detained and held against their will inside the barn.

"They said they were with the FBI, but how am I supposed to know if they're telling" the truth or not?" Adele said, smiling, feigning ignorance.

Sheriff Stinson couldn't get up and off the phone fast enough.

"Alright...don't do nothin' else. I'm on my way," he said and hung up.

"Jesus fucking Christ," he thought, heading out the door of the sheriff's office, practically sprinting to where he'd parked the squad car.

Sheriff Stinson fell in love with Adele, *The Witch,* the first time he saw her, and the two started having an affair soon afterward before Adele's husband committed suicide. Coincidentally, Sheriff Stinson's wife committed suicide as well. Nobody ever investigated the two suicides to see if they were somehow connected, but people there in Richmond County sure thought suspiciously of it. With both spouses out of the way, Adele and Sheriff Stinson were free to do whatever they wanted.

***

"My sister likes you."

"What' you mean 'she likes me'?" I asked, not really believing it. Little did I know, Adele had a thing for working black men, the kind who had good jobs and professional types.

"She likes you," said Angel, again, but this time with more emphasis, adding body language, eye contact, and matching facial expressions. This was after we'd finished our meal and had gotten back on the interstate, I-95 South.

"The thing is...okay," said Angel, taking in a deep breath, allowing it to come out slowly while gathering herself to be sure what she said came out in just the right way in which she wanted it told.

Turning in the seat to face me, she said, "Adele's my sister, and I love her dearly, but man, she's weird...I mean, really weird."

"Okay, but why are you tellin' me? I'll probably never see her again."

"Oh, believe me, if she wants to see you again, then she will, I'm sure. She has a way of makin' things happen."

What Angel said made me laugh. "You make it sound as if your sister has some kind of magical powers or something."

"She does. You'll see."

***

With the lights on the squad car flashing and with the siren wailing, Sheriff Stinson was able to drive fast enough to get there at Adele's farmhouse in less than fifteen minutes, a thirty-minute drive usually from downtown Richmond. By then, the men from the FBI were hot, and not just from the warm temperature inside the barn, but from how fuming mad they were for being detained and held against their will at gunpoint.

Especially Special Agent Wheeler.

"I want her ass and the rest of these hillbillies arrested, NOW!!!" he said when Sheriff Stinson got there to amend and relieve the situation. Sheriff Stinson waited until all three special agents cooled off before he gave them their guns back, though.

"It was a mistake, gentlemen, and a big misunderstanding."

"BULLSHIT!!! We identified ourselves as the FBI, and these assholes blatantly disregarded our authority."

"Ah...what authority is that?" Adele asked, still unwilling to back down, "The authority to come out here and pull your weapons on me for no apparent reason and without a warrant? I'd say you were violating my rights as a private citizen, sir. And not only that, this is private property, which gives me the right to protect it and whatever's on it."

The exchange between Adele and Special Agent Wheeler would've gone on if Sheriff Stinson hadn't intervened.

"Can I ask why you're here?" Sheriff Stinson finally asked after tuning in on the last remark Adele had made, which did make a lot of sense. The special agents obviously didn't have a warrant, and if there wasn't any real emergency to create probable cause, then Adele was right; they had no business there in the first place, definitely not in the manner in which they came and did with guns drawn. Therefore, Adele and the men who worked for her had all the right and reason in the world to not only protect themselves but also to handle the situation aggressively, just like they'd done.

"It's their right," he thought, taking Adele's side.

Also, not only was he there to help and protect Adele, but the remark about Adele and her men being *Hill Billies* wasn't taken very well by Sheriff Stinson either. The rural communities in the hills of Virginia were home to him. It's where he'd been born and raised. And although he was black, he considered himself *"A tobacco-chewing, moonshine-drinking hillbilly"* as well.

"Look, this woman, Angel Clark," Special Agent Wheeler said, looking over at Adele, "Her boyfriend and a few of his friends robbed a bank in Philadelphia yesterday morning. And we're here to confiscate evidence that was taken."

Adele laughed.

"And you find this funny?" asked Special Agent Wheeler, still showing how mad he was.

What he said made Adele laugh even more.

"Sir," said Sheriff Stinson, intervening once again. "She's not Angel Clark. She's Adele Madison, Angel Clark's twin sister."

It wouldn't be until thirty minutes later before the whole

confused disorder was figured out. By then, Sheriff Stinson had made calls to the FBI in Richmond, who called the FBI in Philadelphia as well as the Philadelphia Police Department, the ones who were actually in charge of handling the Philadelphia bank robbery case.

And Special Agent Marks called Governor Olamay, who also made some calls, calls that defused the whole thing quickly.

"Enough of the bullshit. NOW FIND THAT FUCKIN' PHONE!!!" he yelled and told Marks after calling him back.

In the end, no charges were brought against Adele and her men for *interfering with law enforcement* or against special agents Wheeler and Marks or Harry Burgess for the illegal way they came onto Adele's property, brandishing weapons.

However, the laptop and tracking device that Burgess had left in the car had a beat on the phone again.

"According to the reading I'm getting, the phone and the girl are both headed south on I-95. They've just crossed the North Carolina state line and are nearing the City of Rocky Mount."

Chapter 11

Club Rolex, Miami

Speakers outside and inside the famous strip club were blaring the new upbeat song by the rapper *Pee Wee Long Way.*

"Jump inside the pussy, and do the backstroke.

Smokin' on the gas, I got strip throat.

I've been goin' housin' on the West Coast.'

She tryin' to read my future like she's Cleo."

Regardless whether I enjoyed or understood the song's lyrics was irrelevant because the rest of the rap crowd was singing along and enjoying them.

It was a special night at Club Rolex. The ex-stripper/rapper, Trina, was being honored and celebrated with a countdown, a countdown to midnight which would be the beginning of the actual party, celebrating the celebrity's fortieth birthday. She and her entourage occupied the whole VIP, as did her ex-boyfriend Lil'

Wayne and his group, which featured professional athletes like Edgerrin James, Udonis Haslam, and Antonio Brown. But everybody else there in the club was celebrating it, too, including Wild Boy Reed and his entourage.

"I heard you have been in the studio tearin' it down," said the guy standing next to Wild Boy Reed, a record producer from the Atlanta area.

"Yeah, somethin' like that," said Wild Boy Reed, smiling from ear to ear, being modest and shy. Regardless of the stage name he'd been given, or the hard-core rap lyrics that were on all the songs he made, Wild Boy Reed was a brilliant, humble young guy.

He was the youngest of four boys, all brothers from Overtown, one of the worst areas in Miami. Two of his brothers had fallen victim to gun violence and were killed on the streets, and a third brother was serving a life sentence for the murder retaliation.

The boy's parents, Joseph and Betty Mathurin, both Haitian immigrants from Port a Prince, lacked education but did the best they could trying to raise the boys. It became heartbreaking later, only being able to stand by and watch helplessly as the streets engulfed and took their sons away, all but *Jean Claude Mathurin*, aka Wild Boy Reed, whom the older brothers would oftentimes insist on staying home...*keepin' out the way.*

"Go back in the house, you're too young for this!!!" they used to yell, telling him when Wild Boy Reed would come outside anyway late at night, crying about being left behind. Little did he know what the brothers did actually saved his life. His way of thanking and repaying them was by rapping about their rough, rambunctious, hell-raising life experiences.

"Here, try this on," the record producer from Atlanta told Wild Boy Reed, handing him a new gold Rolex wristwatch.

"No, since in bein' here in the Rolex if you don't actually own one," he said, smiling while showing off to Wild Boy Reed the Rolex watch he was also wearing.

"And there's a lot more where that came from. All you gotta do is come to Atlanta and sign with us, 'Big Money Records."

Chapter 12

After driving all day and well into the night, we were finally crossing the South Carolina, Georgia state line near Pooler, Garden City, and the historic city of Savannah.

Angel was also awake again and hungry.

"I'm starvin'. Can't we stop and get somethin' to eat? And what about a room? I need to shower and freshen up a bit," she said, sounding innocent and sweet like a child. Anything she asked, I probably would've done it for her.

A few minutes later, she and I were at a Waffle House, ordering coffee and patty melts with hash browns and scrambled eggs.

"Make those to-go," I told the waitress, thinking that if I got a room, Angel could shower, and after eating, I could shower, take a nap and sleep for a while.

A moment or two later, the waitress was back with coffee in Styrofoam cups.

"You want cream and sugar?" she asked. Both Angel and I did, and a moment later, the waitress was back with that too.

In no time at all, the cook was done making what we ordered, and the waitress was putting it all in a bag. With how well we were being served, in my opinion, both the waitress and the cook deserved a big tip.

I noticed another couple leaving, a couple in their mid-twenties. Two other guys around the same age were with them. The girl was pretty and actually looked a lot like Meagan Good. The guys were all dark-skinned, had dreadlocks and gold teeth, and wore their pants low, hanging slightly below the waist with the waistband of their underwear showing.

The fashion they sported, called initially *jailin' or baggin'*, was stereotypical of today's black male youth, a look initially inspired by that of a prisoner after having his belt taken away in jail. In most cases, this would make the prisoner's pants droop and sag, exposing the waistband of whatever underwear or shorts he might've been wearing underneath. Not what I would consider a good example or role model to follow as a fashion trend.

The combined look of the couple and their friends was also like a group of people who'd been in jail or prison before, definitely not a group you wanted to cross or meet in a dark alley.

I watched them all walk out and leave, talking and laughing the whole time. A moment later, the cashier rang us up, the total for what Angel and I had ordered. I'd just handed her the money for it and told her to keep the change when outside, a hail of bullets from what sounded like an automatic weapon cut down the four youths. A dark color SUV sped away moments afterward.

The SUV was already parked in the parking lot when Angel and I drove in and got there; I noticed because the parking lot was well-lit, and the SUV he was driving looked a lot like mine, a black Chevy Suburban. I also saw that the engine was still running, and a man was sitting in it behind the steering wheel. I thought nothing of it, though, thinking he left the engine running because he still had the air or the heat on and might've been hungry like we were and sitting there waiting for somebody to come out with the food they'd ordered. It wouldn't have been unusual if he was.

It turns out the crew inside the restaurant were rival gang members from Savannah, *Bloods*. Rival to the guy outside in the dark-colored SUV, which was a Savannah *Crip* gang member.

But not only that, the girl was playing both sides, cheating on the guy in the dark-colored SUV with the guy she was with in the restaurant.

The guy driving the SUV had followed them there and then waited and watched the whole time while they were all inside, eating and enjoying themselves.

I'm sure the more he watched, the more it pissed him off, especially with the way they were all talking and laughing; the girl even kissed the guy she was with.

When they came out, I thought to myself, *"That's probably why the girl was shot and killed first, and then the guy she was with."*

Gun violence and death were at a high amongst black youths in America primarily due to gang involvement and participation.

"We're killing ourselves," I thought an hour later after Angel, and I had been questioned by the police and then finally given permission to leave.

We drove away from the scene saddened and traumatized, watching while the two black youths, after being put in large black bags, were both loaded in the coroner's van to be taken to the Chatham County morgue.

The other two had already been rushed away to the nearest hospital emergency room. The chances of whether they would survive or not were up in the air...*a fifty-fifty chance,* we'd been told. Silently, I said a prayer, hoping the two would survive.

Chapter 13

Angel and I rode in silence for the next ten miles or so until we got to an exit that had hotels and gas stations that I saw were brightly lit and still open at two in the morning.

"You alright?" I asked after pulling up and stopping at one of the gas pumps.

"Yeah, I'm fine," Angel said, although I knew she wasn't. Since the shooting, she'd cried twice, and even then, at the gas station, she still looked sad and had tears in her eyes.

"I'm gonna go inside and grab a few things while we're here," she said and got out, slamming the door of the SUV behind her.

I used a credit card at the pump and had already filled the tank by the time she came back out, bag in hang and drinking from a bottle of orange juice.

There was a Days Inn across the street.

"You still wanna take a shower?" I asked, treading lightly so as not to upset or make her cry again.

"Yes. I just bought deodorant and soap," she said, forcing eye contact and a smile, "...and a toothbrush and toothpaste," she said, taking both items out of the bag, holding them up so that I could see them, "And last but not least, a charger for the phone." The battery in the new iPhone had gone dead. It wasn't until we'd gotten halfway to Florida that Angel finally realized or even thought about the phone needing a charger.

"Okay, you ready then?" I asked, turning the key and starting the SUV.

"Yep, ready when you are," she said, sounding like a sweet little girl again. I admired the effort she gave to make things better by trying to come to terms with what we'd just seen, which was for sure one of the worst scenes I'd ever witnessed. However, it showed by the look in her eyes that everything wasn't alright and that she needed some kind of relief or comfort. I was thinking, *"She might even need more time to cry,"* and if she needed a shoulder to cry on, then I was ready to be there for her.

***

I ate while Angel showered and was already asleep by the time she'd finished and came out of the bathroom. The rattling of the bag and what was inside of it woke me, and that's when I noticed that she was finally trying to eat something. I also noticed the only thing she had on were panties, pink lace panties that, as far as I could tell, were practically see-through.

"Oh God," I heard myself say in thought, feeling the arousal and excitement of wanting her in bed with me.

Instead of lying there, gawking, teasing myself, I rolled over and covered myself completely, something that included covering my head and face.

The room I'd gotten was a room with double beds. But just as I'd fallen asleep again, I felt Angel's warm, soft body slide in beside me into the bed I was already in.

"Oh God," I heard myself say again. Even with being half asleep, the arousal and excitement were back with twice as much intensity.

With our bodies being so close, her being in bed with me, how could I resist? And I didn't. A moment later, the pink lace panties were gone, and so were the socks and underwear that I'd had on. And then Angel and I were making love. Deep, passionate, profound love. Love that seemed to take me to heaven, love that seemed to last for hours, which might've only lasted twenty minutes actually, but twenty intensely good minutes.

Afterward, with me still panting and out of breath, Angel began to tell me everything that had happened since Jake had come home with the money from the bank robbery. Telling me about it would serve as another form of relief for her.

"They shot straight through the door and just killed him," Angel said, crying again. I could feel the tears with her lying practically on top of me. I also felt it when she took in and let out a deep breath.

"I managed to get out through a window and down the fire escape," she said, taking in and letting out another deep breath. "But then these two guys came after me. They looked like cops, but cops aren't supposed to just shoot people like the way they shot Jake."

"Why they came after me, I still don't know. But one thing's for certain, they're not somebody I wanna trust. So, I kept running, feeling that I had to get even further away from them, somewhere out of town. That's when I called, askin' Giorgio for money. Thank God he sent you," she said, reaching up with soft lips that found and kissed mine.

"But then, now this. I swear, I just wanna go someplace peaceful and quiet for a while, where nobody's gettin' killed."

"And you think that's what you'll find in Miami?"

"I don't know. I'm just confused," she said, starting to cry again. This time I put both my arms around her and held on tight. She lay there and just cried until, eventually, she cried herself to sleep. It was late, well after three in the morning, and I fell asleep too.

It wouldn't be until around eleven O'clock, well after the sun had come up later that morning, when we were wakened again by the lady coming to clean the room.

"Housekeeping," the lady outside the room said after knocking hard on the door. "Are you guys gonna stay over?" she asked.

Yeah!!! was what I wanted to yell out and say so I wouldn't have to move right away and could continue to enjoy the magic I felt laying there with Angel still sleeping beside me.

But unfortunately, I couldn't. With very little time to spare, there were still too many miles left to drive and lots of work to be done. If too much time passed, then the trip I was making to South Florida would be in vain, a waste. Wild Boy Reed would more than likely already be signed.

Chapter 14

"Heyyy. Chill out, will you!?! Don't be confused. What we did last night was just sex, nothin' more," Angel said, now with a frown on her face, quite a contrast from the night before. This was later that morning in the parking lot after we'd checked out of the hotel, just hours after we'd made love.

What set it off was when I opened the passenger side door of the SUV for her. When she stepped up to get in, I made the mistake of leaning over towards her, thinking I might get a kiss.

"And why in the hell did I wanna do that?"

The next thing I knew, she was frowning and asking me to stop. It might've helped, though, if I had bought a toothbrush at the store the night before, as Angel had done, and used it before we checked out of the hotel.

"At least then I wouldn't have had such bad breath," which I thought might've been the problem.

"Okay, alright. I apologize," I said, feeling like a sap again for the ridiculously lame way I was starting to lose control, reacting from feeling so happy and passionate.

"Silly of me for actually thinking we'd turned a page and had become a couple," I thought, quite embarrassed.

After making sure she'd gotten in and after closing the door behind her, Giorgio's voice came into my head again, telling me.

"See, I told you. Never fall in love with a stripper. They're heartless and way too much trouble."

Regardless of being the dweeb that he was, Giorgio was also a smart ass and didn't mind voicing his own selfish opinions. But in this case, I should've listened to what he told me.

"It's too late now, though," I thought while getting in on my side of the SUV. I was already there, in love...*and because of it, I had already gotten my feelings hurt.*

***

The whole time that night at the hotel, the phone never did get charged. Angel forgot and left it and the bag outside on the backseat of the SUV and was unwilling to get it later, not after showering and getting all comfortable. And now, with me driving us out of the parking lot, she was finally able to plug into a charging port, one of the ones inside the SUV, supplying the phone with immediate power.

After turning it back on, only then did she see messages from Adele, something about the FBI being there in Richmond.

"Wow. At Adele's farmhouse?" Angel wondered.

One message was more specific, more to the point, and a lot

more alarming.

"Call me as soon as you get this. Two guys, one black, one white, both of the FBI, were here looking for you."

"For me? Shit," said Angel, worried and fearful again, and suddenly with more tears in her eyes, wondering, *"How did they know how to find me?"*

"What's wrong?" I asked, noticing the alarm on Angel's face and the sudden change of demeanor. She seemed tensed all of a sudden, more perturbed than she was already.

She didn't say anything at first and just sat there, trying to hold the tears back. Not for long, though. The message from Adele was too much to hold in.

"Those two guys, the ones I told you about. The ones who came after me. I think they were at Adele's. She says they're FBI."

"Shit," I said, wondering what the hell I'd gotten myself into, "If they came to Adele's looking for Angel, then chances are they're probably lookin' for me too by now. But for what?"

***

"Maybe it's time to put out an APB on them," said Special Agent Wheeler, "We know what kind of vehicle she's riding in and who's driving it."

"What, and alert everybody on the eastern seaboard about what the hell we're doin'? Nah, I don't think so," said Marks, awakening on the passenger side. Burgess was still asleep in the back. They'd driven all night, stopping only to get gas and to switch drivers.

"No, I think we should stick to the plan. Find this uncle of theirs in St. Augustine first, see if she might've gone there. Hell, we just missed them in Richmond. She's runnin' scared.

"Where else do you go when you're afraid and feel like you have no place else to go? You go home or to the place you consider home.

"Let's go there first. If she doesn't show, then let's put out an APB. We wanna try to do this shit as quietly as we can first, though."

"Okay, you're probably right," said Wheeler, in agreement with Marks. St. Augustine was only fifty or so miles away,

"Another twenty, thirty minutes, we'll be there," he thought, leaning back in the seat, making himself comfortable again.

"Let me know when we get close, will you? Gonna sleep some more."

Marks looked over and laughed. In less than thirty seconds, Wheeler was fast asleep and snoring.

"I've never seen anybody fall asleep as fast as this guy," thought Marks.

Chapter 15

Pete and Irene Clark's house sat at the very end of Mooring Road, the only house on Mooring Road actually, on the very edge of Flagler Beach, where St. Johns County met with Flagler County. Pete built the house himself.

Condos and other oceanfront properties, including luxury townhouses and apartments, were scattered further down Flagler Beach. But Clark's two-story house stood alone just the way Pete Clark had imagined it would always be.

At eighteen, Pete, a Bostonian from Southie, an old Irish neighborhood in Boston, signed up for the army and fought proudly in the Vietnam War. He loved his country and would've died for it had it been necessary.

As a high school sweetheart, he married Irene, the woman he loved then *and will always love.* That's what Pete used to say to anybody who would listen.

Together they had two sons; Michael, the eldest, and Bobby,

who both now lived nearby and worked for the St. Johns Sheriff's Department there in St. Johns County, St. Augustine.

However, recently Pete's mental condition wasn't the best anymore...*not nearly what it once was, and deteriorating rapidly.*

After Vietnam, he was diagnosed with PTSD, post-traumatic stress disorder, also called post-traumatic stress syndrome, a mental condition affecting those who might've had a very shocking or brutal experience in their past...*like a traumatic experience of war.*

At times the disease caused Pete to suffer from depression and anxiety. But lately, the depression and anxiety attacks had gotten worse, happening more often than ever. He was at a point of suffering flashbacks like those from him being back in the war again, even after taking the prescribed medications.

Nonetheless, his wife and sons let him hold on to an old shotgun...*a gun used to protect the house.*

But Pete was a collector, and the rest of his extensive arsenal of weapons was put up and hidden from him. Twice he'd fired shots from an M16 out the back door towards the water, claiming the house and property were under attack and being invaded from the beach.

Coincidentally, that night, neighbors further down the beach reported seeing something similar...*strange lights and what sounded like something distinct, crisp rumbles of thunder out over the water, along with a strange patch of fog,* not the typical rain storm.

One neighbor even described it as possibly being some kind of bizarre, unearthly phenomenon.

She never said anything about it, but Angel happened to be awake that night too. Earlier that evening, before they had all gone to bed, she'd stolen a cigarette out of Aunt Irene's cigarette case and, while smoking it, had a window opened upstairs...*to let the smoke out.*

She saw what Pete saw too.

Pete and Irene were Adele and Angel's uncle and aunt, Pete being their father's older brother. As kids and even as young adults, Adele and Angel spent a lot of time there with *Uncle Pete,* Aunt Irene, and their two sons, Michael and Bobby. With Adele and Angel's father already dead and after their mother passed away, the two really had nowhere else to go. Pete and Irene both insisted they come to live with them there in St. Augustine. They did, and eventually, the house there on the beach became to be home for Adele and Angel too.

Michael and Bobby, and Adele and Angel as first cousins, were all very close to one another, especially Bobby with Adele and Angel. They were all around the same age, three years younger than Michael, and went to the same Junior and high school together.

At times Adele and Angel, as twins, would switch identities as a prank to fool people. But not Bobby; only he could tell the difference between the two identical twin sisters. There were times, even as adults, when the two sisters would trade places. One guy Angel dated caught on to what they were doing. Angel had gotten a fresh scar once from a spider bite. When they switched places, Adele didn't have the same scar. The guy didn't mind. He called it getting a double treat.

Once, when they were kids, Pete and Irene hosted a family

gathering there at the house on the beach in St. Augustine. Well, although they were just kids, about ten years old, Adele and Bobby stole liquor and got drunk. Nobody knew until Bobby got sick and threw up all over the living room. The two were grounded for a month, Angel too, to keep her and Adele from switching places.

Great memories! The three would sometimes laugh and say, now, as adults, thinking back on some of the mischievous things they used to do. It wasn't a wonder why Angel wanted to stop and see them, especially after fearing her life might be in danger.

So, when Special Agents Marks and Wheeler both showed up asking questions about Angel, it wasn't a wonder either why the special agents were greeted with cold shoulders and sent away so quickly, almost to the point of being treated rudely.

"Can I help you?" Pete asked, out in the driveway with a rugged and unfriendly look on his face, the shotgun not far away, leaning against the wall in the corner of the garage. Pete didn't like visitors much, especially not the authorities of the law.

"Most of them, law enforcement officers," he thought, and believed from past experiences, *"...abuse their authority, acting more like fuckin' bullies."*

Michael and Bobby had both become deputy sheriffs, but other than them being his sons, Pete never wanted anybody else from law enforcement, even on the property, for whatever reason. This was after Frank, Adele, and Angel's father, Pete's younger brother, were arrested and sent to prison.

"For fuckin' nothin'," Pete used to say, "...for nothin' but killin' a man who deserved it," he would say, talking about the man who raped Angel.

According to Pete, *what Frank shoulda' done after he shot him was woke the son-of-a-bitch up and kill him again, twice.*

Special Agent Wheeler was the one who spoke first, answering Pete's question.

"We're here lookin' for Ms. Angel Clark," he said, taking a few more steps, coming a little closer to Pete.

"And who the fuck are you?" Pete asked, taking the two special agents by surprise with the use of straightforward, blunt profanity.

"An old man with a smart-ass mouth," thought Wheeler, without taking another step further towards Pete.

He and Marks both looked at each other, sharing a glance, but before either could say a word, a sheriff's squad car pulled up, and Michael got out. It quickly became evident to the two special agents that the way Michael looked and what he said a moment later only showed a younger version of the older man already there talking to them.

"Gentlemen, can I help you with anything?" Michael asked, recognizing Marks and Wheeler both as law enforcement officers immediately.

"They're here lookin' for Angel," Pete answered and told his son.

"And she's not here," he then told Wheeler, and Marks, hoping to cut things short, sending the two special agents on their way.

"FBI," Wheeler and Marks both said while holding up their badges and identification cards to Michael as if that might've made a difference.

It didn't, and Michael asked, "Why're you here lookin' for Angel? She doesn't live out here," he said, hoping to get to the bottom of things quickly and then sending the two special agents on their way.

If it was human help that Marks and Wheeler were expecting as fellow law enforcement officers, then they were both wrong. Michael's loyalty was to family first.

"We're investigating a bank robbery that happened a couple of days ago in Philadelphia. We know Angel's boyfriend was involved. And we believe he might've given her merchandise taken from the robbery. We're here to get it back, that's all," said Marks in a calm voice, hoping to simplify things and sway Michael's decision to help them.

Well, it didn't.

"So, she's not a suspect or actually wanted for anything?"

"No," said Marks.

"And the three of you," Michael said, including both Wheeler and Harry Burgess, "...came all the way down to St. Johns County in Florida to retrieve or confiscate merchandise taken from a bank robbery that happened in Philadelphia."

"Correct," said Marks.

"What is it that Angel is supposed to have that was so important you guys drove all the way down here to get back?"

"A cell phone. It belongs to the governor's wife; the First Lady happened to be in the bank the day it was being robbed. On the way out, Angel's boyfriend took it."

"Uh-huh, I see," said Michael, thinking what Marks just told him was *some bullshit.*

"If an APB had been put out, then his office, the sheriff's office would've been called and notified, etc."

Having heard about enough, he asked the special agents.

"You have a number where you can be reached?"

Marks produced a card and then wrote on the back his name and the number of his cell phone.

"I can be reached at this number anytime, night or day."

"Okay..." said Michael, taking the card.

"I'll be sure to call if she shows up."

And with that, the conversation was over.

"He won't call," Marks said once they were back in the car.

"Sure, he'll call," said Wheeler, backing out the driveway and going around the sheriff's squad car Michael had arrived in, "He'll call, and then he'll have our asses arrested once he has it processed and find what's hidden on the First Lady's fuckin' cell phone."

Chapter 16

"Sorry about earlier," said Angel, reaching over to touch my arm ever so gently.

"Oh, hell naw...not after hurtin' my damn feelins'," I said, snatching the arm away before looking over, smiling at her, which made Angel laugh and smile too.

"I know...I'm terrible, right?" she asked, still with a smile on her face.

"I woke up with a bad headache this mornin' and wasn't feelin' good at all. I still shouldn't have taken it out on you, though."

"Yeah, and I probably should've bought a toothbrush," I said sarcastically in my attempt to smooth things over, taking some of the blame for what happened.

What I said made Angel laugh and smile again.

"I'm sorry, alright?" she said afterward, making my heart skip a beat again with the way she looked at me with soft, gentle eyes, generating more passion than I could've ever imagined possible.

"Alright," I said, all choked up inside...and all was forgiven.

It seemed, after that, in no time at all, traffic had increased, and cars were moving a lot faster. And looking over both sides of the interstate, houses and businesses had multiplied and seemed to be stacked everywhere. That's because we were in Duval County.

"Jacksonville, Florida, the largest city in the country," I said, just to make conversation, which it did...Angel responded almost immediately.

"I thought New York was supposed to be the largest city."

"Yeah, New York is the largest city, the city with the largest amount of people in it. But Jacksonville is actually the largest city, land-wise."

"Huh...I never knew that, not even after growin' up around here," said Angel, impressed, showing admiration of, interest and respect.

"You're not the only one. You'd be surprised; there's a lotta other people who don't know it either, even some of the other people who live around here."

"Yeah, I'm sure," she said, back to feeling good again.

***

One of America's other largest cities was Philadelphia, the largest in the state of Pennsylvania and the fourth largest in the country. Unfortunately, violence was at an all-time high in Philadelphia, with murders and other violent crimes and attacks happening almost every hour of the day.

Even with police officers working around the clock, putting in more and more overtime, barely taking days off, and presenting a great show of force on the streets, still, *nothing seemed to get any better.*

Gun control, the only sensible answer, was never even considered, at least not by a large majority of those in the U.S. Senate, filled mostly with our country's elite conservatives. These were the same politicians thought to be overbearing in their argument to keep the gun rights law of the second amendment intact. Therefore, mass murders and other violent crime rates continued to escalate, not just in Philadelphia but over the entire country.

"Governor Olamay...a seven-year-old boy was killed here in Philadelphia last night. He was tucked and buckled in the car seat behind his mother, just as he was supposed to be while she drove them home. A stray bullet came through one of the rear doors and killed him.

"A similar incident happened a few nights ago when another child was killed. He was at home in bed. And yet another one a few days before that.

"Can you see a pattern developing here, sir? I mean, about the way our children are being murdered and killed?" asked Kadisha Muhammad while at the governor's most recent press conference, hinting at what she thought was needed. "Gun control...not a very popular subject amongst our politicians these days."

Kadisha, a young female political science major and recent graduate of Rutgers University, happened to be a Black Muslim, people of the religious faith of Islam who were very much a large part of the black community in Philadelphia.

Kadisha also happened to be new on the staff of news reporters for CNN. Even so, being a new reporter for CNN didn't stop Kadisha from being bold, asking questions she thought needed to be asked, tough questions, questions nobody else wanted to ask.

In fact, she was already building an astonishing reputation with local politicians as one to avoid if they didn't really want to be exposed for having not already found an answer or solution for these types of obvious problems Kadisha's questions were about.

"A fuckin' militant," thought the governor about Kadisha and the way she did her job.

The First Lady, Elaine Olamay, who liked and admired the courage of Kadisha Muhammad, stood behind and just to the right of the governor. It was a joy seeing her husband on the hot seat. It brought a smile to her face for both the admiration of Kadisha Muhammad and for the agony the questions Kadisha asked brought to Governor Olamay.

"How dare she ask me some shit like this? She's tryin' to make me look foolish, that's why," the governor thought and assumed, all along thinking about the upcoming primary in the next gubernatorial race for Governor of Pennsylvania, his third.

He needed the black vote; therefore, with the hottest topic of any being gun control, supposedly the cause of violence in the two largest Pennsylvania cities, questions like the one Kadisha asked would eventually have to be addressed and answered.

"It's a pattern that has to stop," the governor quickly spoke up and said, stalling for time to think of a more appropriate way to answer the question both prompt and correctly.

They were at the Robert F. Kennedy Convention Center, a

building that held over ten thousand people. And the place was packed, filled to capacity until it left with standing room only.

"Look...the violent death of any child is unacceptable and won't be tolerated. My heart goes out to all those mothers, fathers, and families who've lost these kids. And I can tell you this, a new task force is being formed as we speak to combat just those kinds of instances of children being murdered and killed."

"Again, I won't tolerate it, and those responsible will be brought to justice."

"Thank you," said the governor, cutting the press conference short, walking away from the podium and down off the stage.

A barrage of questions was spewed by other anxious reporters and even from a few private citizens in attendance, questions all ignored by the governor.

"Sir...you still have about ten minutes left," his chief of staff whispered and said, meeting the governor at the bottom of the staircase.

"What, are you kidding me? Like hell I do," said the governor in full stride, heading backstage, out of earshot range of anybody besides him and his staff who might be listening.

"You must not have heard what that bitch just asked?"

"Yeah, I heard. But I also heard your response, which was quite brilliant actually, beautiful," said Bill Gray, the governor's loyal chief of staff.

"I'm sure the ratings of our entire campaign rose with your response."

"Yeah, but I lied, Bill...there is no new task force meeting 'as we speak,' or one that's even being formed at all to investigate the kids who were killed."

"You're the governor...form one," said Governor Dillon Olamay's chief of staff, making it sound easy.

"What's the big deal? It's not the first lie you've told as governor," thought the chief of staff.

"I'll keep it in mind," said the governor.

"Has anybody heard any more from Marks and Wheeler?" he asked, changing subjects.

"No, not today. We know about them being in Richmond, Virginia, a day ago, but that's it."

"Yeah, Richmond, don't remind me...I had to call in several favors yesterday just to smooth things over down there, all because those two idiots allowed themselves to be taken hostage while whoever this other bitch got away with the phone again."

"Why're they makin' this so hard? It's a simple job...find and retrieve the phone."

"Excuse me for saying, sir, but I think what the problem is, you sent the wrong people to get the job done."

"Oh really? And you know somebody better?" asked the governor.

The chief of staff smiled and responded, "Yes sir, I sure do," and was about to say more before the governor cut in and cut him off.

"That's enough, Bill, don't tell me. I don't wanna hear about it.

Just get it done. I want that phone and all the incriminating evidence on it destroyed by nightfall."

"Yes sir," said the chief of staff before punching in and dialing a number on his own personal cell phone, not the unsecured phone issued to all staff members.

"Hello," he said while walking away, leaving the presence of the governor. "Yeah...the job I told you I might have for you? You're on," is all he said to the person on the other end, before he hung up...waiting for a response wasn't necessary.

Hiring *The Ghost,* the name given to the person the governor's chief of staff, had just hired and talked to on the phone, was a bit of an extreme.

The Ghost was actually a hired killer, an ex-CIA operative gone rogue after being wanted in nine countries, including the United States, for all kinds of bombings and contract killings.

The reason the governor's chief of staff hired him was that regardless of anything, one thing was for sure...The Ghost never failed an assignment. Hiring him almost guaranteed the job would be done.

"If the girl who had the phone, or the guy she was with, if they were both killed...then so be it," thought the chief of staff.

Chapter 17

While driving away, away from the house and beach on Mooring Road, Special Agent Wheeler passed another St. Johns County sheriff's squad car, Bobby coming to check on Pete, something both of Pete's sons had started to do once a day. Pete's last anxiety attack left him incoherent and disconnected from reality, so much so that not even Irene could calm him down.

After hearing Pete yell and shout, a couple, neighbors taking their usual walk along the beach, called the sheriff's department and reported hearing what they thought was a domestic disturbance there at the house, which was why now the brothers took it upon themselves to visit every day just in case Pete suffered another such attack.

It was passing the second vehicle, a black Chevy Suburban, though, that really got the attention of the three special agents.

"That's them," said Harry Burgess from the back seat with the laptop open and the tracking device activated. He'd gotten a positive reading from it. "The phone, it's in that vehicle," he said, turning in the seat, watching anxiously as the SUV drove by.

***

Angel was on a call with Adele.

"Finally," thought Adele when the call first went through and was answered.

"Alright, okay," said Angel, with Adele yelling and practically screaming through the phone.

"Adele, calm down, will you," Angel said to not only Adele but as a reminder to keep herself calm as well while listening to what Adele had to say about the men from the FBI who were supposedly pursuing Angel about the phone Jake had given her.

"That damn new iPhone you're so in love with," Adele told her, "...that's what they want."

"Angel...we gotta be very careful, dear. I normally have a hunch for these kinds of situations. But with these two, I never saw it comin'."

"Alright...okay," said Angel, finally showing a little concern.

The whole time I watched in the rearview mirror as the car we'd just passed made a quick U-turn in the middle of the road. Two of the men I saw inside of it, one white, one black, fit the description of the two men Angel had described and told me about. *The same two Adele was now on the phone warning her about.*

A moment or two later, two sheriff's squad cars came into view; both were parked at the house up ahead of us.

"Angel's Uncle's house."

Bobby and Michael were both inside the house, saying hello to Irene, their mother. It was Pete who came out of the garage to meet us when we drove up. He was carrying a shotgun.

"Uncle Pete," Angel said, getting out in a hurry so Pete would recognize and see that we were of no threat to him. I got out too and walked around the SUV, out in plain view.

"Angel, honey...is that you? Oh, thank God," he said, lowering the barrel of the shotgun, smiling at Angel when she came over to hug him, obviously very glad to see her.

The girls, Adele and Angel, his younger brother's daughters, were Pete's pride and joy more so than even Bobby and Michael were, his own two sons.

"And I'll always love 'em," he'd say so everybody would know, "...love 'em 'til the day I die," and he would.

It was seeing the return of the car that Special Agent Wheeler was driving that set Pete off.

"Quick, get in the house," he said, raising the barrel of the shotgun again.

Pete's son, Bobby, was just on his way back out of the house when the first shot went off,

BOOM!!! a loud shotgun blast.

And then, other shots were heard fired from a semi-automatic handgun.

***

Special Agent Wheeler jammed on brakes, put the car in reverse, and burned the rubber backing the car up, but not before

Special Agent Marks leaned out and returned fire from the passenger side window.

From the back seat, Harry Burgess watched as the old man with the shotgun fell...he'd been shot. And then, a man in uniform, a deputy sheriff, returned fired...a bullet came through the windshield and out through the back of the car, barely missing Harry's head.

"What're you doin'?" he asked, now on the verge of panic. "I thought we were just supposed to be gettin' the First Lady's phone back. Not having a gun battle with members of a Florida Sheriff's Department."

"We are here to get the phone back. At least that's what we're tryin' to do," said Marks, scrabbling to get out even before the car had stopped. Harry Burgess watched him flank right, positioning himself to get off a better shot.

***

Irene had just come out of the kitchen and stepped into the garage.

"Pete!?! Is everything alright?"

"Mom...go back in the house and call an ambulance, QUICK!!!" Michael yelled after coming outside to find Pete on the ground, suffering from a gunshot wound. He'd been hit in the upper left side of the chest, more near the shoulder area.

"Awww hell...I'll be alright. Just get the son-of-a-bitch that shot me," said Pete, looking up at both of his sons, who were helping to get Pete behind one of the squad cars.

"Mike, Bobby...don't trust 'em. Those two are crooks," Pete

said about Marks and Wheeler. "Don't believe a damn thing they tell you."

Bobby looked at Michael.

"One of them just got out of the car, and he's now tryin' to flank us," he said, looking at Michael for advice on what to do next...Michael had served a tour in Iraq and had experienced gun battles before. It was Bobby's first time.

"Just keep your head down," he said, first to Bobby. "You too, Angel," he said before shifting his stare towards me, "All of you."

Next, he had the door of his squad car open, the microphone of the radio in hand with the loudspeaker on.

"SPECIAL AGENTS MARKS AND WHEELER. I'M SERGEANT CLARK OF THE ST. JOHNS SHERIFF'S DEPT... WE MET EARLIER. YES, I KNOW WHO YOU ARE. I JUST GOT OFF THE PHONE WITH YOUR BOSS IN PHILADELPHIA. YOU'RE NOT EVEN SUPPOSED TO BE HERE. AND NO, THEY KNOW NOTHING ABOUT YOUR PURSUIT OF MY COUSIN ANGEL OR THIS PHONE YOU'RE SUPPOSED TO BE LOOKING FOR. GIVE IT UP...GO BACK TO PHILADELPHIA. THEY'RE WAITING WITH QUESTIONS FOR YOU."

Michael paused a moment; that's when we heard the approach of sirens.

"An ambulance with paramedics, hopefully, here to help Pete," we were all thinking, *"...and more help from the St. Johns Sheriff's Department."*

It wasn't long until we heard a car door slam shut, followed by the sound of a car burning rubber on the road while driving away fast in the opposite direction.

"I think that's them," said Bobby, somewhat relieved; you could tell by the look on his face. "They're leaving," he said, even more relieved.

"Yeah, they're gone," said Michael, relieved too that the ordeal was over. A moment later, he looked over at me.

"You need to get her outta here," he said to Angel, looking at her now too, "...at least until I find out what the hell is goin' on," he said, more as a plea for us to cooperate.

What we'd just gone through, *a shootout with the FBI*, had left us all confused and shocked and in a state of wonder. And time to think and figure things out was what we all needed.

"Something I can't do, worryin' about you," thought Michael, but already worrying about Angel.

Angel was leaning over Pete, crying.

"No...I'm not goin' anywhere," she said, with a tight grip on Pete's hand, feeling sorry for him...Pete had passed out.

"This is all my fault."

"No, it's not your fault. You didn't shoot anybody."

"No, but I lead them here," said Angel.

Michael ignored the remark. He looked at me instead.

"Where're you headed?" he asked.

"Miami," I said, enjoying the idea of leaving.

"Okay, look...I want you to take Angel with you," said Michael, with his eyes and body now leaning forward toward me as they do in football, like he was a quarterback about to call a play, and we were all in a huddle.

"There's a cove about a quarter mile down the beach. It's got grass and weeds growin' up around it, but you'll still see it. There's also a path that runs down beside it. Don't worry; you can drive the SUV down the beach; it's allowed. And what you're riding in will fit the path," he said, noticing the skepticism plainly shown on my face.

"Take that path...it'll empty out into an orange grove by old man Gulley's property," he said to Angel, who he remembered was familiar with the area and knew some of the same neighbors that he knew.

"From there, a dirt road will take you around the orange grove and lead you to another road similar to this one," he said about Mooring Road. "You can take that road back to the interstate, I-95, and from there, you can get to Miami. Angel, call us when you get there, you hear?" he said, bearing down a cold stare at her and then at me. "I want you to keep her safe until I can find out the hell's goin' on."

"Okay," I said, and Angel gave him a nod.

"Okay, now go before they all get here," he then said about the ambulance and other law enforcement officers that we all knew were coming.

Michael wasn't taking no for an answer.

"Don't worry about Dad; he'll be alright...it's just a flesh wound. Now go," he said again, mainly to Angel, who was still reluctant to leave. She eventually listened and allowed me to help her up and back inside the SUV.

On the way around to my side of the SUV, Bobby caught up to me.

"Take care of her, you hear?" he said, with cold, piercing eyes, a look that could indeed kill.

"I'll blame you if somethin' happens."

He and I had never met or even said a word to each other besides the threat he'd just made, but the feelings were mutual. I felt responsible and would carry the burden of responsibility from then on. As far as I was concerned, Angel was mine, mine to love, cherish and take care of, and from that point on, I made a promise that I would die before I ever let anything happen to her.

After that, for some reason, a thought came to me, a thought about something I'd once been told. *"Never make a promise you can't keep."*

As we were leaving, riding along the beach, we both looked back and could see the ambulance arriving, along with two other squad cars, both from the St. Johns Sheriff's Department. The car with the men in it from the FBI was back as well. I realized then that the promise I'd just made to myself about keeping Angel safe might very well be put to the test.

Chapter 18

We met four off-road vehicles speeding towards us on the beach, the drivers all with matching shirts, shorts, helmets, badges, and sidearms. Law enforcement officers from three different counties were all assigned to patrolling the luxurious area and expensive oceanfront properties between Daytona and Flagler Beach.

To me, it was obvious where they were all going. *To Pete's house, in response to a report that shots had been fired.*

I even expected them to stop me in my SUV to ask questions. But to my relief, they passed right on by...*didn't even look twice at me.*

Those were the only other vehicles I saw riding shoreside that day, but tracks in the sand let me know that different cars and SUVs did sometimes, in fact, travel on this area of the beach as well. It made me feel a whole lot better, though, when we made it to where the cove was. And sure enough, the trail Michael had described and told us about was there just as he said it was.

Angel recognized it right away.

"Yeah...turn in here," she said when I got to exactly where we were supposed to be, "and watch the fence," she told me.

"What's left of a fence," I thought after noticing a barrier made of rotted wooden posts connected by rusted fence wire. Sections of it even had boards connecting the posts instead of wire.

"This was probably once used to keep animals in or out, goats or cows maybe," a thought told me.

There weren't any recent tire tracks going through the path or even a gate connecting the fence, so I imagined how old it might've been.

"...very," I thought after turning in, hitting a few unseen bumps.

While driving through, Angel smiled and said, "There was once a gate here, and when we were kids, we used to come through it all the time to go steal oranges.

"We got caught one time, though. And when the property owner, Mr. Gulley, took us home and told Uncle Pete about it, he grounded us for a whole month. After that, we never went back to steal again from Mr. Gulley's orange grove," she said, on the verge of crying again from being reminded about Pete and more great childhood memories that were spent there with him.

"The war messed him up, and he's gotten a little senile, but regardless, he's always been a great guy," said Angel about the uncle she loved and admired. "And he's always taken real good care of Adele and me."

That I thought was obvious by the way he fired his gun without hesitating, all to protect Angel. It didn't matter if the men he'd fired on were with the FBI or not; protecting Angel was his one and only priority. I envied Angel for having somebody who cared so much, a father figure who loved her. I was eleven before I ever even met my father or any of my uncles, and I never felt such given love.

***

October 10th, 1961, was the year I was born at Phoebe Putney Hospital in Albany, Georgia. My mother, at seventeen, had to be rushed there at two in the morning, all alone. I could only imagine now how scared and terrified she must've been, just as she must've been with the challenge of trying to raise me all alone. She did the best she could, I'm sure, which for me was never enough.

I was a bastard child and lived up to it in every sense of the word. Nevertheless, I was to become a hero, at least that's what my mother thought and hoped for, a wish compelled and urged on by calling me Trent, after the only other hero she'd ever known. Yet, in the upcoming years, signs would show that I was to become anything other than a hero, more of a villain if anything, a scoundrel on the cusp of becoming a criminal.

My intentions were to rebel and cause as many problems as possible, and for no good reasons other than just because I could. I knew of the questionable origin I'd come from and took offense, blaming those around me…*mom, grandma,* the only people who actually cared about me.

The bad seed was planted early on from so many times hearing Mom curse Dad, cursing him for not being there as a husband, a companion, or as a caring parent. The problem with me, though, was that I didn't just blame him. I blamed her, too, for us being so poor and without all the things I wanted or needed, and for whatever other reason, for anything I could think of.

So, with the blame being shared, the idea was to cause as much trouble as possible and bring them no happiness at all from me. *"Them"* being the key word, though, which, as it turned out, was more unfair and one-sided than I'd realized. The selfish gain of satisfaction was all I cared about. And so, the plight began.

All through school, elementary, junior high, and high school, the relished thought of having a dad escaped me, even after we'd actually met. When we spent time together, I felt genuinely unloved by him; it was more like being pitied or like an old debt being paid and that his two younger sons from the woman he'd married were the actual prize. There was no bond that was ever formed, no love or friendship, just an obligated relationship based on being blood relatives that made us father and son, nothing more.

The relationship that formed between my brothers and I was good. We actually became friends. But even then, amongst the thoughts of me and the rest of the family, I was still the bastard child, something that even until this very day bothers and hinders me.

"Trent Walker, the hero? I doubt it, not in the realm and scope of this lifetime and world," I'd say sarcastically back when I was a much younger man.

"But my, how things have changed," I thought, looking over at Angel, the woman I'd so quickly fallen in love with. For her, I was willing to do just about anything, whatever it took to keep her safe, even if it meant dying.

"I love you, baby," I said, in words that only I could hear, but meaning it sincerely, with all my heart and soul.

"I guess mom was right after all, huh," I thought with my eyes

back on the road again. *"They usually are."*

Chapter 19

"GET THOSE MOTHERFUCKERS OUTTA HERE, OFF THE PROPERTY, AND AWAY FROM MY FATHER'S HOUSE!!! THEY'RE THE ONES WHO SHOT HIM," Michael yelled and shouted about Special Agents Marks and Wheeler being there on his father's land and property. Pete had already been put in the ambulance and taken to a hospital…. He would've objected too.

Marks yelled back.

"YEAH!?! YOUR FATHER WAS THE ONE WHO SHOT AT US FIRST. THIS WAS AFTER WE IDENTIFIED OURSELVES AS FBI SPECIAL AGENTS!!!"

After Pete had been shot, on Mooring Road, while driving away from the scene, Special Agent Wheeler passed an ambulance and then several more cars from the St. Johns Sheriff's Department. However, seeing the additional law enforcement officers made him decide to come back and face them.

"We're the fuckin' FBI. We should be there on the scene, not runnin' away from it," he thought, gaining confidence, feeling confident and more conscious of having the power of authority regardless of all the existing laws they'd broken.

After calling Governor Olamay, the governor insisted they go back and explain what happened too.

"...To clear yourselves, dummy," he told Marks.

Wondering, *"How did these two busters ever become special agents? Aren't you supposed to have a certain level of COMMON SENSE at least!?!"*

"Fuckin' idiots," said the governor after the call was over.

"Where are they?" asked Wheeler, after looking around, not seeing the black SUV, the Chevy Suburban Angel, and the phone were supposed to be in. Angel had put the phone back inside the bag, so the reading and signal that Harry Burgess got earlier were no longer being received.

"WHERE THE HELL ARE THEY!?!" he shouted when he thought Michael hadn't answered fast enough.

"GO FUCK YOURSELF, YOU HEAR!?! FUCKIN' SON-OF-A-BITCH!!!" said Michael, pointing a finger, returning the profane gesture of shouting and yelling obscenities.

He looked and saw two fresh, new bullet holes in the fender of his new squad car the county had bought for him.

"Asshole," he said, not happy about that either.

Bobby and Irene had both gone along in the ambulance with Pete to a hospital in Jacksonville. If not, if he'd stayed behind, chances are Bobby would've shot Marks and Wheeler, especially Marks, after he'd shot his father. Like Pete, Michael and Bobby both had terrible tempers, especially when it came to the well-being and safety of family, those they cared about and loved. And Pete...well, Pete was Bobby's hero.

Michael was a lot like Pete. He grew up fast and was always off somewhere on a quest with friends, some of the other older boys, and especially the girls...Michael had a fond liking for girls at an early age. He even ran away once, leaving his younger brother behind to fend for himself.

All along, though, Pete was there for his younger son, befriending and hanging out with him. The two would go fishing, to mostly all the ball games, to Boy Scout meets, everything a kid like Bobby wanted to do.

And now that Pete, more or less suffering from dementia, was at times all alone in what they thought and considered unreal worlds bordering insanity and saneness, Bobby didn't plan to abandon or leave him either. Without a second thought, he would die or kill for Pete too.

"Tell me...What's really goin' on with these two?" another deputy sheriff asked in a conversation with Harry Burgess, who all the while had been hanging back, distancing himself from all the hoopla and excitement that Marks and Wheeler seemed to be creating.

"I don't know and really want no part in it," he said, giving somewhat of a confused answer.

"How do you know you want no parts in it if you don't know what it is that's goin' on?" the deputy sheriff wondered.

"Chase Bloomberg," he said, with a hand stuck out after laughing a while.

"Harry Burgess," the two shook hands.

After that, within another five minutes or so, Deputy Sheriff Chase Bloomberg knew everything Harry Burgess knew about why the two special agents were there. It seemed to be such a coincidence that Deputy Sheriff Chase Bloomberg also happened to be with the internal affairs division of the St. Johns Sheriff's Department there in St. Augustine and served as a liaison between the St. Johns Sheriff's Department and the FBI.

Half an hour later, a call was made to the main office of the FBI in South Florida, specifically to Special Agent Maria Lopez Montero. Special Agent Lopez Montero's parents had both come from Cuba in the '70s. Since then, Maria Lopez Montero had taken advantage of the American dream, becoming a special agent for the FBI.

"Chase...Wassup?" she asked, with a casual tone and attitude.

"Was just thinkin' 'bout the love of my life and wanted to call to say hello, that's all."

"Bullshit," she said, walking away from those in and around her desk and office so the conversation with Chase could be more private. The two were once an item, and the usual topic of their conversations, when it wasn't about a case they were working on, was about sex.

"Haven't heard from you in a while. You must be horny," she said, feeling a sense of sexual excitement starting to grow and stir inside of her as well.

"I'm always in the mood for you," said Chase, meaning it wholeheartedly with thoughts of their last encounter. They drove and met at the halfway point between Miami and St. Augustine at a hotel in Vero Beach, a rendezvous planned just for sex.

The two broke laws in every county along the way, driving unnecessarily fast at high rates of speed, at times over a hundred miles an hour, to get there in a hurry, which they did, arriving at about the same time there at the Vero Beach hotel.

Once inside the room, like animals, Maria ripped and tore his clothes, and he ripped and tore at hers, leaving every inch of the room battered and littered with everything they were wearing, shoes, guns, and badges included.

An hour later, they were both asleep, spent and exhausted from having some of the best sex ever.

"If you're calling to entice me about another rendezvous, I can't. We're busy working on a case," Maria said, while actually hoping to be persuaded otherwise.

"No, actually, that's not why I'm calling at all. We've got two hotshot special agents here from Philadelphia. They claim to be working on a case, a bank robbery. But after making a few calls, I've found that the case was actually handed down to Philadelphia PD, and these two aren't even on it."

"Anyway, one of them just shot a civilian, the father of a colleague of mine, supposedly in an attempt to retrieve a cell phone that was taken in the robbery."

"Just wanted to see if you could check them out, see if they're on the up and up."

"Somethin' about 'em don't seem right. To me, they seem dishonest, like they might have an agenda that has nothin' at all to do with enforcin' the law."

"Oh...and they brought a technician with them. He's not too comfortable with them either."

"Ok...what's their names?" Special Agent Lopez Montero asked, making her way back inside to where her office and desk were.

"Special Agents Marks and Wheeler...Mutt and Jeff," Deputy Sheriff Chase said, ending with joking about what he thought of the two special agents.

"You wouldn't happen to know their badge numbers, would you?" Maria asked, on a whim, hoping she'd be lucky, getting the necessary information that would help her find the two special agents quickly.

"No, but what I can tell you is that they don't seem very well-liked in Philadelphia. Nobody I talked to seemed to have anything good to say about 'em. You might wanna give the office there a call."

"Okay, will do. I'll get back to you when I've got somethin'."

"Okay, thanks, I'd appreciate it."

"Oh, and by the way...what color panties are you wearing today?"

"None...now bye Chase, before you get us both in trouble again," the special agent said, smiling ear to ear before hanging the phone up, but also remembering the trouble they'd gotten into. The Vero Beach police were called during their last encounter about the room they wrecked, and calls were made by the state police about both of their cars which were reported speeding unnecessarily along I-95 through several counties. A reprimand was given to both Deputy Sheriff Chase Bloomberg of St. Augustine, as well as Special Agent Maria Lopez Montero of the FBI.

Chapter 20

"How is he?" Angel asked after calling Bobby's phone to get an update on Pete's condition. We'd only gotten about fifty miles away on I-95, near the exit for Daytona Beach.

"They got him in surgery to remove the bullet. But he'll be alright. Thank God it wasn't nothin' too serious."

"What about Aunt Irene? How's she holdin' up?"

"She's fine. I'm here with her."

"What about you? How are you holdin' up?" Bobby asked, knowing how much Angel loved and admired Pete.

"Almost as much as I do," he thought.

Angel pretended to laugh. She just wanted Bobby to know she was fine.

"How am I holdin' up? Let me see... Where should I begin?" she said after the laugh was over. But she now sounded as if she was suddenly in a serious thought, which she was.

"I'm a little pissed off, confused, hungry, you name it," she said in a way more humorous than serious.

Bobby laughed too.

"Yeah, same here," he said, agreeing with everything she said, even about being hungry.

"It just don't seem right...all of this about a damn phone? Maybe I should just give it to 'em," said Angel, sounding more like a person on the verge of giving up, unwilling to stand by and allow anybody else to be hurt, thinking, *"It's just not worth it."*

"I bet there's somethin' on it, somethin' they don't want anybody else to see."

"No, I don't think so. At first, I thought that too, but I've gone through it, and there's nothin' on it besides a video of the bank bein' robbed."

"I'm sure the FBI wouldn't be so pressed about a recording of a simple bank robbery recorded on somebody's personal cell phone. Hell, the bank's got plenty of cameras everywhere and got them set to record things at every angle," said Bobby, thinking back on some of the training films he saw during his time at the police academy, films on previous bank robberies.

"No, that's not it. It has to be somethin' else."

"Maybe you should bring it in and let one of our techies look at it to see if there's something hidden inside it."

"Yeah, maybe I should," said Angel, agreeing, but at the same time having thoughts unwilling to give up the phone, the new pride and joy in her life.

"No, never," she thought. Thinking, *"If I give it to 'em, I won't ever get it back."*

"Angel...gotta cut this short, the doctor just came out to give us an update. I'll call you back, alright?"

"Alright," said Angel, hesitantly, not wanting to hang up and break the bond of talking to someone so close to her, the bond of a family member, somebody she knew she could trust.

"Call me back," she said, just before hearing the click of the phone hang up on the other end.

"How is he?" I asked, concerned about Pete too. We'd never actually met, but I already admired him.

The whole time, riding along down I-95, I never noticed the silver Mercury Grand Marquis riding along, a few cars behind us. The guy driving it sure saw me, and stayed a few cars behind, following us.

Chapter 21

Elaine Olamay, the First Lady of Pennsylvania, was formerly Elaine Ellenwood of Portland, Maine. Elaine's family descended from a wealthy, aristocratic pedigree that may be traced back to the Royal family of England, which might explain why the Ellenwoods were still treated like royalty in Maine.

They'd just finished dinner and were entertaining guests. Elaine just happened to be drunk.

"A governor tough on crime, my ass. Yeah, right," she said, laughing while sipping on even more liquor than she'd already had, making fun of the governor's slogan.

A governor tough on crime. A governor for the people.

"And which people are you the governor for, Dillion, huh? The gay people?" she asked, throwing insult after insult at the governor, hoping to provoke him.

The governor, a tall, Rock Hudson look-alike, a very handsome, all-American white guy who did turn out to be gay, just sat there with his face and neck both turning red. He almost crushed the glass he had in his hand from being so angry. Yet, he remained silent and in control, refusing to respond or say a word in response to the insults.

"You're nothin' but a pompous ass, a ferry," Elaine said, continuing with the insults.

"What's the matter, don't you even like pussy? Have you ever? Or is it that you can't get it up anymore? I can get some Viagra if that's what you need."

When he still didn't say anything, Elaine finally decided to give up.

"Oh, what's the use?"

"He won't fuck me, and he won't hit me. He won't even get mad about what I'm sayin'," she said, turning to face their guests.

"He's too damn scared," she said, laughing again and slurring each word she spoke terribly from feeling the large liquor volume she'd drank...*way too much apparently,* or so it seemed. Nonetheless, she was the only person in the room who caught the punch line.

She eventually got up and walked away, stumbling while she did it, bouncing off walls and everything, even the staircase railing, until she made it upstairs and to her side of the house. She wouldn't come out again until early the following day.

"Elaine's not well. Please forgive her," said the governor in an attempt to clean things up.

The guests were there to donate large amounts of money to the governor's campaign fund. It would've been tragic to allow Elaine to ruin things and change their minds. Unfortunately for him, that was precisely what Elaine was trying to do...*ruin his career.*

In the meantime, while the governor was down in the luxurious dining hall of the governor's mansion, busying himself with damage control, his wife was upstairs making a late-night phone call.

"Marty, How much longer do I have to carry on with this shit?"

"Until I tell you to," said the voice on the other end of the phone, the voice of Marty Blair, the director of the FBI. "Until we catch the son-of-a-bitch," he said, suddenly with regret, mellowing a bit, undoing the soar attitude he had towards the First Lady, feeling somewhat sorry for her. Unfortunately, what the governor said about Elaine was true; she wasn't feeling well. She had been diagnosed with stage-four cancer, wasn't expected to live much longer, and was sometimes forced to endure and deal with unbearable pain.

However, an investigation against the governor revealed a blackmail scheme by the First Lady. She was blackmailing the governor himself, a crime that could've sent the First Lady to jail.

The phone that Marks and Wheeler were so desperately trying to get back had a video recording hidden on it, a recording of the governor and his two flunkies, the same two FBI agents, committing murder. The person who was killed happened to be one of many young men the governor had had a love affair with, Ryan Mitser, a convicted sex offender who decided to steal a stack of the governor's one-hundred-dollar bills. The governor's pride wouldn't allow Ryan to get away with it. So, he sent Marks and Wheeler after him.

They brought Ryan back to the governor's ranch one night when the governor and Elaine were away from the governor's mansion to have a country barbecue, entertaining other guests.

The governor, Marks, and Wheeler were all roughing the guy up when he slipped and fell, hitting his head on a steel beam. In reality, the governor swung a shovel and hit Ryan; that's what made him slip and fall.

Anyway, after hitting his head, he died immediately. The death was never reported. Instead, Marks and Wheeler tied cinder blocks to the young man's body and dumped it in the ocean.

Without them knowing it, Elaine had managed to sneak up on them and filmed the whole thing, even them tying cinder blocks to the young man's dead body. Elaine planned to use the recording as a tool for blackmail.

The day the bank was robbed, the First Lady was there to deposit a ten-million-dollar check written out to her by the governor, a payment in exchange for the phone with the recording on it. Nobody figured the bank would be robbed and the robbers would take the phone.

Nevertheless, the more prominent part of the FBI's investigation wasn't just about Elaine Olamay, the governor, or the rogue FBI agents. After the case had been discovered and investigated, the case against them was straightforward with their eminent arrests.

The bigger fish, though, was *The Ghost,* the killer the governor's chief of staff had recently called and hired to get the phone back, a man wanted for several other murders...a man who had eluded the capture of the FBI for an entire decade.

Nobody even knew what he looked like, not even the governor's chief of staff, who, so far, was the only person known actually to have a number to reach him.

Well, the chances of catching *The Ghost* had finally gotten a lot better. The only problem was stopping him before anybody else got killed.

"Whoever the girl is who has the phone, he won't just try to retrieve it from her," the director of the FBI explained to all those present and involved in the investigation.

"So, remain alert at every turn, gentlemen. This one could be a bit dangerous and serious," the director insisted.

According to previous investigation experience, the killer never left a surviving witness who could identify him, "...which is how he's never been caught," explained the FBI director. And leaving a living witness wasn't part of the plan this time either.

Chapter 22

"Finally," I thought, after the fifth straight hour of driving down I-95, relieved to see Miami, Florida, road signs like the one that said:

Dade County, introducing the area in and around the fabulous resort/retirement city of Miami, Florida.

Home of 'The U,' The University of Miami, and the legendary Miami Dolphins, the only NFL team in history to complete a professional football season undefeated, winning every game of the regular season, the playoffs, and the Super Bowl of 1972. Hats off to each player on the team, the coaching staff, and especially the then-head coach, Don Shula.

And the Miami Heat when they had Dwayne Wade, before and after LeBron James and company.

"They're a Jimmy Butler team now, though," I was thinking, going back to the playoffs in 2021 and '22.

"Are we finally here?" Angel asked, coming awake after a long nap. She stirred once when we were passing through the West Palm Beach area and again when we hit Fort Lauderdale. I was even tempted to wake her and stop in Hollywood, Florida, to see my relatives and an old friend from high school. But the priority was to find Wild Boy Reed as soon as possible.

I had no idea the silver Mercury Grand Marquis was still driving behind a few cars between us at a safe distance.

***

Club Elite, a neighborhood strip club in the *Little Haiti* area of the 2nd and 62nd Street neighborhood, was once known historically as *Lemon City, Little River,* and *Edison.* It is where the historically oldest library in Miami-Dade was located.

The neighborhood was home to Haitian immigrants, exiles, and residents of people from the rest of the Caribbean. A thirteen-foot bronze statue of General Toussaint L'Overture, the father of the Haitian revolution, stood on the corner of N. Miami Avenue and 62nd Street.

Thinking back on it, my family members also had a history in the Little Haiti area of Miami. And from what I remember, not everything about the Little Haiti area was historical or clean.

A cousin of mine in Albany, Georgia, Marvin Edwards, a semi-drug kingpin, decided to come to Miami to buy drugs. He wanted to start with a kilo of cocaine first to test the waters of doing business with the Haitians before working his way up to truckloads.

People he knew in Albany directed Marvin to Little Haiti and a body shop on NE 2nd Avenue near 62nd Street. Supposedly the owner was someone Marvin could do business with, a guy who could sell and supply him with whatever he wanted or needed...*regardless of the amount,* he was told.

Well, as it turned out, the body shop's owner wasn't on the up and up at all, and instead of doing business with Marvin, he had Marvin killed. They took the thirty or so thousand dollars Marvin came to Florida with and split it amongst themselves, giving a cut to the friend who directed Marvin there in the first place, a guy in Albany who was supposed to be a good friend.

Angel and I would later pass the exact spot where Marvin was gunned down and killed.

***

"So, what you gon' do, Reed?" Roc, a longtime friend of Wild Boy Reed, asked.

"About what?" asked the young rapper.

"Come on, man, don't play. About the contract they want you to sign," Big Money Records offered Wild Boy Reed ten million to sign with them.

"I haven't decided yet."

"Whata' you mean, you haven't decided yet? What's there to decide?" Roc asked him. They'd all been born poor and raised in one ghetto or another in Miami, and signing a ten-million-dollar contract meant they would all prosper and live a much better life.

Desmond Franks, aka Roc, and his twin brother, Raymond Franks, had grown up with Wild Boy Reed. They were his brothers now that his real brothers were dead or in prison. At six foot three, two hundred and forty pounds each, they were Wild Boy Reed's bodyguards, protectors, best friends, and business partners. And both would gladly die if necessary to keep anything from happening to him.

Club Elite was their club, their personal hangout. And with Roc and Ray there, along with the other ten or so guys who were always around, the safety of Wild Boy Reed was secure.

"We can't keep expectin' to get away with bein' gangsters, sellin' dope forever, Reed," said Ray, the real brains of the outfit. Roc was in charge of security, but it was Ray who made sure things were running smoothly. And to date, as a group, their primary source of income came from the sale of cocaine, marijuana, meth, and x-pills, ecstasy, which were all illegal substances that came with hefty Florida prison sentences if and when they were ever caught.

"An eventual outcome," thought Ray. *"It always comes down to doin' time when you're doin' wrong."*

Roc and Ray were a few years older and started out as friends of Wild Boy Reed's older brother, Michel, who was given a life sentence for killing the two guys who killed the two other Mathurin brothers. During the trial, Michel made Roc and Ray promise and swear that they would never let anything happen to his younger brother, Wild Boy Reed, a promise Roc and Ray planned to keep.

"With ten million dollars, we can go legit and never have to do anything illegal again," Ray explained.

"Yeah, I've already considered it," said Wild Boy Reed, "I just doubt that they can pay it. And even if they can, I think I'm worth more…a lot more," he said. And he was... Big Money Records was a relatively new company in the industry, a company with limited resources and a limited amount of cash. They planned to go all out trying to sign one man, Wild Boy Reed, an artist who could get them out of the dumps of recognition, and earn them the respect they were hoping for in the industry, something a company like Mix Master Productions didn't have to worry about. They'd done it already, a long time ago.

"Alright, this Chuck Reamer guy…the guy from Big Money Records, says he's leavin' in the mornin'."

"Let him. He won't be hard to find in Atlanta if I change my mind."

"As a matter of fact, here, give this back to him too," said Wild Boy Reed, passing Ray the gold Rolex watch he'd been given, "I'm not one for wearin' a lotta jewelry anyway."

"After thinkin' about it, I feel somewhat disrespected that he'd given it to me as if I could be bought off so easily. The ten mil they're offerin' isn't even guaranteed, and they're only offering a hundred grand up front, that and a Rolex watch."

"Naw, Ray...I'm lookin' for a company that'll respect me and my talent. A company I can grow with and learn from. I'm just not feelin' that with Big Money Records."

"Okay... I hope another company comes along then, so we can change what we're doin' and how we get money."

"Don't worry, that's exactly what's comin', a change, and soon...I can feel it," said Wild Boy Reed, sharing a big smile, spreading optimism and belief, and encouraging his longtime friend.

Chapter 23

"Once you're there, drop her ass off somewhere," Giorgio said, advising me on what I should do with Angel once we got to Miami. And in the beginning, that's exactly what I planned to do. But not now, not after the way I was starting to feel.

"I'll blame you if somethin' happens," those were Bobby's words, Angel's cousin. He wouldn't have to worry about that either...I planned never to let anything happen to her.

"...not ever again. How could I? It would be like hurting myself."

Angel wasn't aware of it, though. At least, I didn't think she was.

"Where are you takin' me?" she asked, remembering what Michael and Bobby said, the part about keeping her safe and not dropping her off somewhere to go strip down to nothing. It would be her dancing on stage with a bunch of horny men watching, throwing dollar bills at her all over again, beginning from scratch.

"First, I wanna get you a change of clothes," I said, coming up with a much better idea, taking her shopping. "Then I need to find a guy called 'Wild Boy Reed,' a young rapper I came down here to sign."

"After that, I figured we could go someplace nice and cozy, someplace we can get a bite to eat, maybe have a drink or two, and just chill for a while."

"What if I don't wanna go someplace nice and cozy and chill for a while?" said Angel, thinking about drugs, wanting to get high again. She'd had plenty of time to recuperate, eating and resting since the night with Jake when they smoked, snorted, and drank as much as they could handle. The Jones of being addicted was coming down hard on her now, though, especially after all the excitement that happened with people around her getting shot and killed.

"Look... You still got these two guys from the FBI after you. And I promised Bobby and Michael I would keep you safe until they figure things out, and that's what I plan to do. So chill, don't make this any more complicated than it already is."

"Okay, but I wanna get high," she said, telling the truth, not bothering to bullshit me with the usual lies a person on drugs would tell. And for that, I respected her and thought I might even consider obliging the request.

"I'll see what I can do," I said, trying to decide what to do next.

"I gotta find Wild Boy Reed first, though, alright?"

"Okay," she said, sounding like a kid again, getting the best of me and my feelings for her. It made me think of the movie *Lady Sings the Blues,* an old classic story about love and hardship, one that Berry Gordy, the Motown mogul, did about the singer Billie Holiday. But we all know how that one turned out... Billy Dee Williams, portraying the role as Louis McKay, was left heartbroken by Billie Holiday, the icon who, while being performed by Diana Ross, died addicted to heroin, much too young at 44 years old.

***

After waking up, Angel first grabbed the phone out of the bag to check for messages. When she did, Harry Burgess was able to get another reading.

"They're in Miami," he told Marks and Wheeler from the backseat of the car that he no longer wanted to ride in.

Everybody knew Harry had a wife and three daughters whom he loved dearly, more so than he did being a technician for the FBI.

"...and more than ridin' with these two clowns, riskin' to lose it all," his thoughts about being with Marks and Wheeler.

"Miami it is," he told them. "When we get there, whether we get the phone back or not, I'm catchin' a flight back home."

To Harry, it felt more like being a part of an illegal vendetta in their pursuit of the girl, more than so trying to retrieve the First Lady's cell phone.

"...somethin' I want no further part of," thought Harry about the present situation and the men he was in the car with. *"They're both too sloppy and unprofessional. And this is turning out to be quite a mess."*

Chapter 24

This time it was Adele who asked about Pete, except she was there in person. How she'd gotten there so fast, nobody knew.

"I got here as soon as I could," she said, joining Irene, Bobby, and Michael at the Jacksonville hospital, in the waiting area for family and friends.

"How is he?" she asked.

"Physically, he's fine, but he won't stop worryin' about Angel. At one point, he became hysterical, goin' on and on about her life being in danger... The nurse had to give him a sedative to calm him down. He's sleepin' now," Irene told her.

"One of the guys who came to the house, Dad claims he recognized and that the guy is a killer," said Bobby.

"They came to my house too. Which one of 'em was Uncle Pete talkin' about? The black guy or the tall white guy?" Adele asked.

"Neither," said Michael, almost as if it was funny, "The nerdy-lookin' guy who sat in the back seat... The guy with the curly red hair. That's who Dad claims is a killer."

Hearing this almost made Adele laugh too. *"He has got to be kidding,"* she thought, remembering the look on Harry's face when the men at her house forced him out of the car. *"Like he might've shit in his pants."*

But then something came to her, a late intuition. Something she didn't feel or think of before. It was the way he looked...*the cold stare he gave when they were leaving.*

"He had the eyes of a killer," she said privately, a thought that suddenly gave credence to what Pete said and was thinking.

***

A call was made to Miami from the FBI Director.

"Special Agent Lopez Montero?"

"Yes sir," the special agent said in answer.

"Marty Blair, Director of the FBI," the FBI Director said as if Special Agent Lopez Montero needed an introduction. She was well aware and knew who he was, just as everybody else in the office knew.

"I'm calling to inform you about your boss, Special Agent Schillers. Unfortunately, his wife has died, and he's been forced to take a leave of absence."

"You're now in charge. Any problem with that?" he asked.

"No sir," said Special Agent Lopez Montero, a smile appearing on her face. She knew Brad Schiller's wife had been fighting breast cancer for years, and it was indeed a very unfortunate situation for

Brad and his family. Nevertheless, a promotion was something Special Agent Lopez Montero had been hoping to get for years.

"...since my first day on the job," she thought.

Well, now her time had come.

"I'm confident you'll do fine," the Director of the FBI said.

"Thank you, sir," was her response.

"Okay... Let me put you up to speed on a situation headed your way," the FBI director told her.

Thirty minutes later, she knew everything there was to know about the case with Angel, the two rogue FBI agents, and all they knew about The Ghost, their main target. She kept to herself about having already started a file on the two rogue agents. She'd also started a file on Harry Burgess and already had an idea about who The Ghost might be.

Chapter 25

Before leaving home, Adele did some things nobody expected her to do. First, she locked herself inside the house and wouldn't open the door for anybody. And then, from the inside, the house was set on fire. Later a gunshot was heard; it was thought Adele shot herself, committing suicide.

The men working for Adele had all gathered and stood outside, demented, helpless, and worried from not knowing what to do. The twelve group members were all gathered around the tree, watching in awe while the house burned. Some were in tears, but then some wore smiles.

The fire department and County sheriffs came out, including Sheriff Marty Stinson. But the house burned down to the ground anyway. And after the fire was out, authorities found remains of a woman, remains thought to have been that of Adele's body.

Furthermore, a trap door was found on the floor, hidden under an old antique rug. The trap door led to a tunnel that extended from Adele's land a quarter of a mile down, where a ladder showed to another trap door that opened inside an old country shed hidden behind an old, run-down house covered in weeds and shrubbery. Nobody had lived in the house for years, a decade, maybe. It was later learned that Adele also owned that particular house and property.

There was an old Ford pickup truck parked outside, and the keys were in it, making it easy for her to get away. Adele obviously had no plans of ever returning.

***

I did everything I could to make Angel forget about wanting to get high. First, we went to Bal Harbor and shopped in stores like Saks Fifth Avenue, Lord and Taylor's, and Bloomingdales, and whatever she wanted, I bought for her.

Next, we went to Miami Beach and ate on the exquisite hotel terrace of Fontaine Bleau, known for housing stars and people of the rich and famous. Right after we'd arrived, Angel waved and said hello when she saw celebrities like Miley Cyrus and Justin Bieber. I waved and said hello too... I'd met them both and had planned to maybe do some work with them one day.

The icing on the cake was when Shaquille O'Neal came by and dapped me up.

"Watch this guy," he told Angel, kidding her about me, "He's a sweet talker," he said, smiling and giving Angel a friendly wink. She was left in awe.

"Havin' fun yet?" I asked, seeing the big smile on Angel's face after the big man had left our table and walked back inside the hotel.

The words wouldn't come out right away, but the positive answer came by how big the smile on her face was and by how many times she quickly nodded her head, so many times I thought she might have a sore neck afterward.

After we both ate a big meal, we got a room and made love immediately once we got inside. In my mind, like the first night she and I made love, she was mine again, the sweet, loving Angel Clark whom I adored... It was after only two days of being on the road with her. The only problem was that Angel didn't feel the same about me. It blew my mind because it was like she had no feelings at all, and sex was just something she did to please whoever the man she was with. Whether things between us would ever change was still yet to be seen.

I thought, *"I can't expect her to be like me and fall in love immediately,"* which was true. *"For her, it wasn't love at first sight. Not at all."*

And knowing this made me want to accept the challenge and never give up trying to make us a couple.

***

I saw it when Angel took the phone out and sent text messages. That was over an hour ago before she and I started making love. She was at it again now and was suddenly about to get out of bed.

"I'm going to go down to the lobby for a minute. You don't mind, do you?" she asked, as if she needed my permission to leave or go where ever she wanted.

"Of course not," I said, watching her get dressed.

A moment or two later, she was gone. All the bags of clothes and things I'd bought for her were still there, but I was still left wondering if she would ever return.

Thirty minutes later, I was relieved to hear it when the door opened again and even more relieved to see Angel walk in and smile at me.

"Hi," she said, still smiling as if the time she'd been gone was a lot longer than just thirty minutes. And although she wore the same clothes and had her hair done the same, she seemed different, like a totally different person, which she was... I didn't know it then, but she and Adele were at it again, trading places, playing their old childhood trick, but this time the trick was being played on me.

Chapter 26

After closing the door and ensuring it was locked, Adele came right over, put both arms around my neck, and kissed me like I'd never been kissed before. The passion I felt emitting from her was unmistakable…the excitement, the strong sexual, romantic feeling. I thought she was Angel, and I hoped she'd finally come around to feeling about me the way I felt about her.

Everything she did was perfect.

I was starting to feel like the happiest man in the world. That was for sure, especially after how she pushed me back down on the bed and the way she started making love to me again...*as if she hungered and craved for more.*

I wanted to ask, "What's gotten into you?" but didn't, refusing to interrupt or spoil the mood, deciding instead *to enjoy it while the fun lasted.*

Thinking, *"She might change on me again later, as she did before,"* ending all excitement and joy.

So, we spent the next two hours in silence, kissing, hugging, and making some of the best love ever, doing the things that two people in love might do.

I eventually fell asleep and didn't wake up until I heard the door open and close again. Angel, the real Angel, was back...*and she smelled just like alcohol and marijuana.*

***

Marks and Wheeler had just pulled up outside and saw Adele leaving the hotel.

"Is that her?" Marks asked, hoping to finally finish the quest of getting the phone back over and done with.

"Yeah, that's her," said Wheeler, holding a picture of Angel up, to compare the two.

"You sure that's not the sister?"

"What are you talkin' about? How could it be the sister?" Wheeler asked, looking over at Marks, a little perturbed.

"We left that crazy bitch back in Richmond, remember?"

"Okay, I just wanna be sure to get it right this time, that's all," said Marks, pulling the car over and stopping it, positioning himself and the vehicle in a way to remain undetected while Adele got in the old Ford pickup truck she'd walked over to. The plan was to follow her to wherever she was about to go and then jump out with guns and badges, catching her off guard and taking the phone away from her easily, or so they thought.

Little did they know that Adele had spotted them in the car the moment she came out of the hotel and had a little something planned for them, too... It would be a rude awakening if they weren't careful. A rude awakening to who she really was.

"...for Uncle Pete," she was thinking.

What Adele had planned for the special agents, they would be lucky if they survived it.

Chapter 27

Angel took three showers and stayed up the rest of the night, keeping me up much of it too with the way she kept walking and moving around. She'd met a busboy in the hotel who knew a guy on the beach who sold meth and marijuana, two substances that had a combined effect on her, which was now nerve-wracking...*she wouldn't be still.*

And there was no more love, affection, tenderness, or passion, all of that left with Adele when she walked out the door.

My only thought about it was that Angel had changed again.

"...gone back to her usual self, just as I thought she might."

However, she did bring back a bit of good news.

"I met this guy downstairs," she said, towel in hand, while drying her hair and flaunting her naked body after the third shower she had taken.

"He told me about a club over on 62nd near 2nd. He said

somethin' about Wild Boy Reed bein' Haitian and that we might find him there since the area around the club is Haitian."

"It's a strip club. You mentioned that Giorgio said Wild Boy Reed likes strip clubs, right? Well..."

"Okay, I'll be sure to remember all of this when the time comes for me to wake up," I said, turning my head away from her and covering it up, but not before sending a message, making sure she knew I was trying to be facetious, and that at the moment I thought she was annoying.

The next thing I knew, a pillow was flying, thrown my way, hitting me square in the head.

"You're awake now, aren't you, smart ass," she said, making sure I knew that she'd gotten the message and the last word in what little conversation she and I were supposed to be having.

Chapter 28

Ford pickup trucks, a popular automotive item in the U.S., were supposed to be among the toughest, most rugged trucks on the market. Being *Ford Tough* was what it was all about, what they were known for, and what made them so popular. It was an advertising slogan Ford Motor Company stood by, guaranteeing their product...*a slogan that was used to sell a lot of Ford trucks.*

Adele had had this one since when she and Bill were first married. She'd bought it used from a guy originally from Italy whose wife had recently died. He decided to leave the U.S. and go back to the old country. When he left, he sold the truck to Adele for a low price. It needed a new motor, so later, Adele had a 5.3 big block motor put in it...*to add more power,* she claimed, and it did, a lot more.

It was the truck she used on and around the farm, the one she drove into Richmond or where ever else she needed to go. She'd often put it to the test and learned everything about it, what it would and what it wouldn't do.

When she put it in gear and took off in it that night with the FBI special agents following behind her, she planned to put it to the test again. That was part of the rude awakening she'd planned and had in store for them, something surely both the special agents were not expecting or were ready for...*at least not from a woman.*

***

"No. This is all wrong," said Harry from the back seat after Marks pulled off, following who they thought was Angel driving the Ford pickup truck.

"I'm gettin' another reading, and it says the phone is still in the hotel."

Marks and Wheeler looked at each other, wondering what to do but thinking the same thing.

"Go after the girl, and put her in cuffs even if she doesn't have the phone."

They also thought Harry's detector might've been getting a false reading. Or that if the girl sold the phone or did something else with it, then they could make her tell who had it and where.

"Look, I'm tellin' you…the girl doesn't have the phone. It's back at the hotel," insisted Harry to what seemed like deaf ears.

"Are you guys listening? Do you even understand what I'm sayin'?" he asked when both special agents still hadn't answered or said anything.

He became much more worried and upset once Marks floored it, and the car they were in started going faster, reaching high rates of speed, almost flying down the highway.

***

Adele left, driving at normal speed down Collins Street, the street with hotels and apartments on one side, and grass and the beach on the other.

The same street that, in many movies, depicts scenes showing one of the most beautiful, picturesque, and photographic views that Miami Beach has to offer.

But once on 79th Street, Adele merged onto the Miami Causeway, Interstate 395. She floored the truck, going as fast as she could across Biscayne Bay, passing Star Island, Dodge Island, and other marine and oceanographic landmarks. She was heading towards I-95 and the mainland, the actual city of Miami.

The causeway inclines, goes up a bit across the water, and comes down on the other side, much like a bridge connecting the other side. Except on the other side, on this particular night, upon entering the city, a traffic jam awaited them. What it would turn out to be was trouble, even for an experienced, veteran driver like Special Agent Marks.

Still with the truck's gas pedal floored, Adele weaved through traffic and miraculously exited to the right on Biscayne Boulevard. Another car got in the way, and Marks wasn't able to follow or keep up. Nor was he able to stop…when pressure was applied, the brake pedal of the car he was driving suddenly went all the way down to the floor.

Impact came almost instantaneously, with them hitting, of all things, a tow truck inching along in front of them. Luckily, the car was equipped properly with airbags, and the lives of all three passengers were spared. All of them, including the driver of the tow truck, only suffered minor, superficial wounds and injuries. All except Harry Burgess…who was thrown forward into the windshield and ended up with a broken neck. He was left to suffer what would turn out to be permanent paralysis from the waist down.

Adele, who then stopped at the exit, waved and blew a kiss at Special Agent Wheeler. He was stunned, but not enough to fail to recognize the face of the one teasing and tormenting him.

"I'm'a get you for this, bitch," he said, regaining more and more sense of awareness, becoming furious as moments passed.

"You can bet your life on it. I'll get you," he murmured.

Hearing the sound of sirens that were for sure heading her way finally made Adele take off.

Chapter 29

"What do you wanna do?" Angel asked that morning, sitting up in bed beside me, using a finger to rub on the lobe of one of my ears.

"Sleep," I said, swatting the finger away like I would a fly or a gnat that was pestering me. "Please, just let me sleep some more," I asked, hoping to get in at least another hour or two.

"Aren't you hungry? Call room service and order breakfast," I said, hoping to give Angel something else to do besides bothering me.

"Anything, just leave me alone," I was hoping and thinking.

Angel found the remote and turned on the television instead. The news channel was on with updates from a special bulletin.

"This morning, around 2 AM, a tragic accident happened on the causeway bridge heading north into Miami. It involved three Philadelphian FBI agents. Two escaped injuries and were only shaken up. However, a third agent was thrown forward from the back seat, hitting the car's windshield. It has been reported that he has been left paralyzed from the waist down. Doctors think the paralysis may turn out to be permanent."

The report caught my attention even while trying to go back to sleep, but I came fully awake after hearing Angel say.

"Oh shit, Adele. What have you done?"

I came out from underneath the covers and asked, "What makes you think Adele might've had somethin' to do with this?"

"Because I know my sister," said Angel, sounding quite sure of what she thought. "After what they did to my Uncle Pete... I'm surprised it took her this long."

***

"Special Agents Marks and Wheeler," said Special Agent Lopez Montero with the now two battered and bruised special agents sitting across from her in the new office she'd just been given. It was the day after the two special agents crashed their car, leaving Technical Advisor Harry Burgess paralyzed.

"What am I to do with you two?" she asked, meaning it seriously.

"You're no longer wanted in Philadelphia, and you're damn sure not wanted down here, at least not by me."

"In St. Augustine, the St. Johns Sheriff's Department might want you, or before it's over, the Miami/Dade Sheriff's Department might even have started searching for you. An investigation is taking place in both counties, which might result in charges being brought against you two."

"So, I'm advising you both to walk carefully from here on out."

It was the beginning of a lecture neither special agent wanted to hear. They were used to always getting their way with the help of Governor Olamay back in Pennsylvania. But the governor hadn't bothered to pick up or answer the phone. Both special agents hoped the governor might still be asleep and not ignoring or refusing to help them.

They kept thinking, *"He can't refuse us; he's involved in this just as much as we are. Hell, we got him by the balls, whether he realizes it or not."*

Neither of them knew it, things had changed, and they'd become just as much of a liability as the phone was. And new orders had been given.

"Yeah, I want them taken care of too," the governor's chief of staff said during the second phone call he'd made to The Ghost. Again, no response was given or was necessary. Without a doubt, the request would be met and upheld. Therefore, the days of both special agents being alive, amongst the living, were numbered and now down to single digits.

Chapter 30

There was no sense in trying to go back to sleep, not after what we'd seen on the news. So, Angel and I did order room service and had breakfast. At least I did. Angel didn't seem very hungry.

Along with breakfast, I also ordered the ingredients we would need for Mimosas, a bottle of their best Moèt champagne, and orange juice. We mixed the two and made the mimosas ourselves.

Angel drank two of them down quickly and burped loudly, something she thought was so funny, probably because they'd made her drunk. I laughed too, but only because she laughed, and I liked seeing her happy, not because I thought burping loud was so funny.

Another bottle of Moèt was ordered along with more orange juice, then burgers and fries a little later for lunch. It rained most of the day, so Angel and I stayed in and had a really good time together. It ended up being a really nice day filled with conversation, relaxation, and some much-needed time to just zone out for a while in meditation.

It wouldn't be until later that night when we headed out to find Wild Boy Reed.

***

It was Friday. Angel and I spent all day lying around inside the hotel room. I didn't realize until later that night when we pulled up in front of the neighborhood club where Wild Boy Reed was supposed to be.

The place was packed, or so it seemed, judging by how many cars we saw parked outside and around it. People were standing everywhere, guys in their best pair of Levi's jeans, Polo shirts, hats, and Timberland boots. Most wore jewelry down with big diamond rings and watches, long gold chains, and medallions with diamonds hanging around each of their necks.

The females were even more fly and attractive with heels and short skirts or dresses on, showing off all their nice legs and thighs. Many of them were also wearing tight tops with lots of cleavage showing off from big boobs, exposing all except the tips of their nipples, tempting and daring all the fellas to look and admire them.

We were definitely at the right place, if we were out to play and have a good time. Those were the thoughts before we got out or stepped inside the area.

"I don't see no other white faces. You gon' be alright with this?" I asked, noticing the look on Angel's face, a look of being in awe, maybe even a touch of fear.

"Oh, I'm fine. Ready when you are," she said, immediately changing faces, exposing a smile and a look more of confidence than of fear. I was convinced.

It was very unlikely that I would find a parking space anywhere nearby. So, I decided to play the part and act like I was a star, double parking the SUV right in front of the place.

All eyes were on us when we got out, especially when Angel got out. She was wearing heels and a short skirt, too, but with a halter top. And she had her hair hanging just right, accenting every aspect of her pretty appearance.

No, Angel was beautiful and stunning.

I was dressed in a grey silk suit ala Michael Corleone in *The Godfather Part II,* a white Versace dress shirt, and black alligator shoes, more like a conservative record producer, which I was, and wanted to be respected as such.

By the time I'd walked around and caught up to Angel, the crowd outside gave way and parted like we were indeed celebrities, allowing us to walk right in. However, once inside, a guy the size of a middle linebacker blocked our way.

"You can't park there. You'll block somebody in," he said, showing us who really had the authority there. It was Roc, Wild Boy Reed's friend and personal bodyguard.

I thought, *"Yes, we're definitely at the right place."*

Giorgio had already told me about Roc and Ray, the twin brothers, telling me that I would have to get past these two guys before Wild Boy Reed would even consider talking to me. I was told that Ray handled business arrangements, but Rocco was in charge of security.

And then, as if on cue, Ray walked over. "How can I help you?" he asked as if it might've been clear to him that I was there on business more so than to hang out and have a good time.

"Trent Walker," I said, extending a hand. Ray took it and extended a smile.

"I'm a producer with Mix Master Production in New York. I'm here hopin' to see Wild Boy Reed."

"Yeah, I know who you are. You worked with Solo Slash and White Boy Nick Spazz. If you could make those two a star, there's no tellin' what you might be able to do with a talent like Wild Boy Reed."

"Yeah, come on in," he said, patting me on the arm and shoulder, smiling from ear to ear, leading the way.

"Give me your keys. I'll have somebody park your ride for you," said Roc. He'd softened, too, inviting us in.

It just so happened, as it turned out, the crowd was there for a celebration, celebrating Wild Boy Reed's twenty-third birthday. As soon as I found out, I insisted that I pick up the bar tab, making it "DRINKS ON THE HOUSE!!!" for everybody.

When Ray grabbed a microphone and announced it, the crowd went wild.

"COMPLIMENTS OF MY MAN TRENT WALKER WHO'S HERE FROM NEW YORK," he said, making a second announcement to tell the crowd about me.

A moment or two later, the crowd went wild again. This time because Wild Boy Reed himself had come out on stage to give us all a live performance.

"LET'S GET THE DAMN THANG STARTED THEN,

Y'ALL!!!"

"WHO DAT WHOOO!?! WHO DAT WHAAATT!?!" he said, going through certain body motions on stage, showing he had swag and phazzaz, and was crunk urging everybody on, encouraging them to get crunk, captivating them before the song even got started.

I could see why so many record companies wanted to sign this guy, why many considered him to be like T.I., or even better than T.I., and the *new king of the south.* He had a great stage presence and was more than just a rapper. This guy was an entertainer and could dominate the music industry…that was for sure. That so with a special kind of charm. And like art, he had a special trait that the crowd loved and found irresistible.

And me *…well, hell, I liked him too, already.*

We met later and agreed we would talk business the next day.

…when we were both calm and sober.

"Tonight's gon' be strictly a celebration, fun, and more fun," he told me, and I agreed. And it was. We got drunk, enjoyed the music, and had the time of our life.

It wouldn't be until when Angel and I were leaving that things turned sour.

Roc brought the SUV back for us, and Marks and Wheeler pulled up behind it. Both FBI agents got out with guns drawn.

"FREEZE, FBI!!!" they said, pointing their guns directly at Angel and me.

In turn, Roc came out, and so did at least ten other guys, and they all had their guns out too, but aimed at the federal agents.

"Who the fuck are you two?" Roc asked them, unfazed by their presence, coming closer to all of us.

"I know all the federal agents here in Miami, including Special Agent Maria Lopez Montero, the one now in charge."

"She didn't send nobody to disrupt our party. As a matter of fact, she called to wish my boy a happy birthday. So, what the fuck are you two doin' here, disruptin' it?"

"No, we're here from Philadelphia. And we're here for her, Ms. Angel Clark," Special Agent Wheeler said. Marks was stunned and afraid. It was the second time in a week that they'd had guns drawn on them, except now, the stakes were much higher being in the rough Miami neighborhood of Little Haiti that they were in.

"Haitians are only loyal to themselves and don't give a damn about law enforcement," the special agent kept thinking.

By then, the crowd and even Roc's men had warmed to Angel. Everybody liked her, especially after seeing how she wanted to dance and mingle with everybody. She wasn't shy, stuck up, or afraid of them.

"Oh yeah? From Philly, huh?" said Roc, coming even closer, getting between the special agents, me, and Angel.

"Tonight, Ms. Clark's with us, and you ain't fuckin' with her," he said with a mean mug now on his face.

The guys there with Roc daringly stepped a little closer as well. One guy, in particular. "Put them damn guns down before I get mad and cap yo' stanky ass," he told Special Agent Wheeler, who now had the barrel of a gun aimed at his head, touching his temple.

"I'll tell you what," the guy said, watching as both special agents lowered their guns. "I got a friend down in the keys. He's got an alligator farm. You wanna go down and see it with me?" he asked, sounding sincere with a sincere look on his face.

What he said made everybody else laugh, though, all except Special Agents Marks and Wheeler, who didn't seem to like the idea of being threatened. The trip to an alligator farm in the Florida Keys the guy was talking about would be a one-way trip for the two special agents.

"Y'all go ahead and take off," Roc said, looking over at me triumphantly, with a faint smile on his face. "These two clowns won't be botherin' you."

With that, Angel and I took off and headed back to Miami Beach. We rejuvenated and energized after realizing we'd made quite a few new friends.

"Don't think I've ever seen no shit like that before, guns drawn on the law. It's definitely somethin' I'll never forget."

"What about you?" I asked, looking over at Angel.

"Uh…uh, never," she said, shaking her head a little before the both of us burst out laughing.

"Serves their asses right," she said, about how the two special agents were disrespected and treated.

Chapter 31

Early the next morning, a sequence of brisk, hard knocks on the door woke us up, Angel and me.

"GO AWAY!!!" I said, in my head, the second time I heard the person knocking.

After having as much as we'd had to drink the night before, somebody knocking hard on the door early the next morning was the last thing we wanted to hear.

But the instructions I gave in my head to *go away* weren't followed, and whoever it was at the door knocked hard on it again.

"Alright, alright...hold on," I said, not wanting to yell in response, or even talk too loudly. *"That'll probably hurt too,"* I thought.

What I needed was some extra strength Tylenol or Excedrin, or maybe some Ibuprofen, but not a lot of hard knocking on the door of the hotel room we were in.

"Yeah...who is it?" I asked after putting on a robe and walking a little closer to the door.

"Special Agent Maria Lopez Montero. I'm with the FBI. Can I come in and talk to you for a moment, sir?" the voice on the other side of the door asked and said.

The name I recalled distinctly and immediately.

"It's the name Roc mentioned last night to the other two federal agents," I thought, remembering it clearly.

The name was mentioned not as if the person it belonged to was an adversary or enemy but as if the female FBI agent might've been somebody Roc had an understanding with and could trust.

So, I was thinking, *"If he felt like he could trust this Special Agent Lopez Montero, then why shouldn't I?"*

It was settled. I'd made a decision.

"Okay, hold on," I said, loud enough so I thought she would hear me. Angel was awake and already up, putting on a robe as well. She looked worried.

"It's alright. She just wanna ask some questions," I said, not sure if that was all the special agent wanted or not. All I knew was that sooner or later, we would have to face them anyway, the FBI.

"So, why not now?" I thought, hoping my intuition about Roc's judgment was right and that the woman on the other side of the door was somebody we could trust.

"Fuck it. Let's get this over with," I said, finalizing my decision to cooperate with Special Agent Lopez Montero.

I waited until Angel was out the bed and standing and was

completely covered with the robe she'd put on. And then I opened the door. And when I did, I found myself shocked. There, standing in front of me, was a younger version of Jennifer Lopez, except this one had a gun and a badge.

"Trent Walker?" she asked, extending a hand, "Special Agent Maria Lopez Montero."

"Please, come in," I said, stepping aside after shaking the hand that was offered to me.

"And you must be Ms. Angel Clark," the special agent said after walking into the room past me.

"Yes, I am," said Angel, smiling while taking the hand offered to her as well, calmer and more relaxed than I'd expected.

"All because of the approach the special agent used in greeting us," I was sure.

Right away, I knew why Roc might've liked and trusted her. Not only did she bring with her a sense of command and authority, but she also brought a sense of peace and tranquility, as if nothing would go wrong with her in the room. I liked her too, already.

"Okay..." the special agent said, gathering herself. "First, I'd like to apologize. I got a call last night about two other special agents who approached you with guns drawn. Those two are not from my office or part of my team, and I had nothing at all to do with it. People in Miami know me for being honest and straight up, with no bullshit or disrespect. If I have a problem with you, I'll tell you...it's a level of honesty and respect that I'm trying to distill in everybody else, too...it's how we'll be able to keep the peace.

"I've heard some other disturbing things about the tactics these two federal agents have used in the past, tactics I don't agree with. However, everybody's different, and people do tend to wanna do things their own way.

"Now, with that said. I hear it's a phone they're after. Obviously, there's something on it, something they think is important enough to kill for. So, if you don't mind, I'd like to see it," she said, turning to face Angel.

The worried look was back as Angel seemed to withdraw and become frightened again.

"Don't worry. I'm not gonna take it from you. I hear it's one of those new iPhones that's so hard to get. I'll give it back…promise. We wanna take a look and see what's on it," she said in a soft, calm voice while even sharing a smile, which made Angel relax again too.

After a moment of consideration, Angel walked over, got the phone from under the pillow, and handed it to the special agent. Special Agent Lopez Montero had brought a technical advisor with her, a technician like Harry Burgess. He even looked a little like Harry, like a nerd.

As soon as she got the phone from Angel, she handed it over to the technician, who got busy immediately. He'd brought a bag with him, a bag that had everything he needed to check and record what was on the phone.

In what seemed like seconds, the technician was done, passing the phone back to Special Agent Lopez Montero, who, as promised, gave it back to Angel.

"We're done," she said afterward.

"Did you guys have any questions for me?" she asked, ready to help if she could or otherwise ready to end the visit.

There was nothing I wanted to ask, nor Angel either.

"Okay, well...here's my card," she said, giving both Angel and me a copy. "Call me if something comes up or if you need me for anything else. Besides that, I hope you two enjoy the rest of your stay here in Miami.

"Oh, and again...sorry about the intrusion last night. Those two seem to be on a short list of agents I'd like to see get fired."

A moment later, she and the technical advisor were gone, leaving Angel and me with a much-needed sense of relief.

Chapter 32

"So, Frank...Whata' we do now?" asked Marks while he and Frank Wheeler sat and had drinks at a local bar on Biscayne Boulevard, not too far from where the accident happened.

"Harry's laid up in a hospital, paralyzed from the waist down, and we're battered and bruised as hell, too," he said, mentioning their own personal injuries. Both were suffering from whiplash with sore necks and backs and sore ribs from how hard they were both hit when the airbags deployed. Marks even had one rib that was broken from where part of his body missed the airbag and slammed hard into the steering wheel instead.

"And, according to Ms. Lopez Montero, we can all but kiss our jobs and careers goodbye. On top of that, now the governor's not even takin' our calls."

"Yeah, the son-of-a-bitch," said Wheeler, still clearly angry and upset.

However, he wouldn't admit it, but what he was upset about,

more so than anything, was how the both of them had been disrespected and rousted once again, but this time by what he called *a bunch of low-life* guys in Little Haiti, guys he considered *nothing but hoodlums.*

But, not even that got under his skin more than being outsmarted and teased about the accident by Adele, whom he thought was Angel.

"Fuckin' bitch!" He would never get over her waving and blowing a kiss at him when they could've all been killed, which made him wonder if how they crashed was even an accident at all, something he and Marks would have to talk about later.

"I still say we wouldn't be in this mess if it weren't for his ass, Governor Dillon Olamay, the undercover fag," said Wheeler, throwing insults to blow off more steam.

"He's the one who actually killed Ryan, not us... He's the one who hit him with a fuckin' shovel and made the guy fall. And when he fell, what happened? He hit his head on a damn steel beam, which killed him instantly. But yet we're the ones about to take the weight of the blame for it."

"Well...you know how that goes," Marks told him. "Every important man has at least one fall guy, somebody who's there to take the blame for whenever they happen to fuck up. This time the fall guys happen to be us."

"Yeah, well, I don't like it."

"Neither do I. But again, I ask, whata' we do now?"

"We continue on and still get the goddamn phone back, or at least try, that's what. And when we get it, instead of handing it over to Governor Olamay, we do what the First Lady did and blackmail his ass with it. Hell, she got ten million. I wonder how much he'll give if we could get our hands on it?"

"Enough to leave the country and get us the hell outta the mess we're in, that's how much," said Marks before taking a sip of the drink in front of him.

"I agree," said Wheeler, sipping from the glass he had in front of him as well. "We haven't gone through all this shit for nothin'. And we still got Harry's trackin' machine, don't we? Yes, we do," he said, remembering all the stuff they took out of the car that got wrecked and into the car Special Agent Lopez Montero gave them to drive.

"So, whata' you say? Let's go find this bitch who's got it and get the damn phone back," said Wheeler, turning up the glass he had, finishing what was left in it in one gulp.

One look at Marks showed that he agreed. He did the same with what was left in his glass, turned it up, and finished it. He also fished around in one of his pockets and came out with a twenty-dollar bill that he left under the glass to pay for both of their drinks, this before the two men gathered themselves and walked out the door.

Neither of them knew it, but Governor Olamay's days were numbered, and so were theirs.

***

Angel and I were having a late lunch when Adele called, giving the bad news that Pete had passed away unexpectedly.

"The doctors don't seem to understand," said Adele, on the

phone all choked up, crying, telling Angel about it. "One minute he was fine, in his bed asleep, stable and recovering as expected from the operation. But then, Aunt Irene got a call this mornin', tellin' her she needs to get back down there in a hurry.

"Unfortunately, his heart had stopped beating. They did all they could to save and bring him back, but at exactly 11:15 this mornin', they pronounced him dead."

I knew the news was bad by the way Angel looked, and then had started to cry. It made me wanna cry too.

"You need to get here, honey, as soon as you can," Adele told her.

"Okay, I will," I heard Angel say before looking over at me.

Thirty minutes later, she and I were done eating and were walking out of the hotel, carrying with us all of our belongings, including the Off Grid Faraday bag. When she and I went shopping, one of the first things I bought was a very nice, very expensive Louis Vuitton, and then a Coach bag for Angel to carry. But for some reason, she still used the old military bag to carry money, the phone, and all her other personal items, which, as it turned out, was a good thing. It gave us a little more time to get away.

Chapter 33

"I tried to clear it up as much as I could, and still, it's not crystal clear, but it's there," said the technician, the one working with Special Agent Lopez Montero. The video of the governor and Special Agents Marks and Wheeler was found, and the technician had it playing on a monitor.

"No, it's not crystal clear, but it's clear enough...you can definitely see Governor Olamay hitting the guy with a shovel before the guy falls and hits his head."

"I think it's enough to get a warrant. What about you?" she asked, turning to face the FBI deputy director who'd flown in from Quantico, the FBI headquarters and training facility in Virginia.

"Yeah, it looks as if Governor Dillon Olamay's goose is cooked. I'll start the process for a warrant right away," said the deputy director.

"What about *The Ghost?* Any good leads on him yet?" he asked.

"I have an idea who he might be, yeah. It's still just a hunch, but I've got men out in the field now, trying to come up with the evidence that might prove my hunch and theory right."

"Okay, good...stay on it. I'll start the process to have the governor arrested, as well as Special Agents Marks and Wheeler."

***

In Philadelphia, the mayor, the chief of police, as well as Governor Olamay himself were all at a press conference following another weekend killing spree. This time seventeen black youths were killed, including five children.

The politicians were all there to face a group of reporters and angry citizens, concerned parents mostly who had already lost a child to gang violence and those who feared losing a child.

Governor Olamay remained in the background and allowed the mayor and chief of police to answer most of the questions.

"It's their city, and they're more qualified to answer," the governor was thinking.

But the CNN reporter, Kadisha Muhammad, was also there, and the questions she had were specifically for the governor.

"Governor Olamay," she said, as a beginning when the microphone in the crowd was finally passed to her, giving her an opportunity to ask questions. The press monitor purposely saved the best for last.

"The last time we spoke, you mentioned something about a special task force that you'd formed and started specifically to combat these types of crimes. What happened to it?" she asked, speaking loud and clear and direct, sure to be heard and understood by the governor, by everybody else there in the crowd, and by all those who might be at home watching and listening.

"And before you answer, sir...understand that I've already spoken privately with the mayor and with the chief of police, and they seem to know nothing about this special task force." Kadisha Muhammad had done her homework and had the governor backed into a corner. Both the mayor and chief of police, two people who didn't like the governor either, were there to dispute any claim on the governor's part about it being a lack of communication or even any level of misinformation about such a task force. He was caught in a lie, point blank, and was being forced to admit it.

"No, unfortunately, the task force was never developed, and for that, I apologize," said the governor, feeling totally disgraced and defeated, unwilling to justify why he did or didn't do it or to carry on with the lie he'd told.

"Thank you," said Kadisha, thinking, *"He is a liar who won't be the governor for very long, not now, not after being exposed."*

And he wouldn't! People in the crowd, as well as the ones watching and listening at home all over the state of Pennsylvania, were already considering how they would vote for a different candidate.

Chapter 34

"Come on in, y'all. How you doin'?" asked Roc with a smile and a hand extended at the door of Ginny V's, a family-owned Haitian restaurant on NE 2nd Avenue in a shopping area of Little Haiti.

Ray was standing nearby wearing a smile, waiting to say hello and greet us too.

Wild Boy Reed was already at a table, though, enjoying what he called his favorite meal, *smothered oxtails with red beans and rice along with fried cabbage and carrots,* a Caribbean meal actually, but one Wild Boy Reed enjoyed just the same.

There was nobody else that I saw there in the restaurant, and it occurred to me that the entire dining area might've been reserved just for us and the meeting we were about to have. The thought I had was confirmed when I saw Roc close and lock the door behind us. It made us all feel a little more comfortable and secure.

"Ummm...that looks good," said Angel after she and I had sat at the table opposite Wild Boy Reed. And it did...it brought back memories of how my grandmother used to make oxtails, a time when everybody in the family would sit around at the table, eating and enjoying themselves.

"The good 'ole days," I was thinking.

"Are you hungry? Would you like to try some?" Wild Boy Reed asked, not thinking that Angel, a white girl from North Florida, had ever even had oxtails before, which she hadn't. The closest thing she'd had to having oxtails was when she had pot roast. She'd never even had neckbones before.

But still, to answer Wild Boy Reed's question, she courageously said, "Yeah, sure, why not," and with a wide smile on her face, which made everybody else laugh and smile too, from just the thought of it, her eating oxtails, that and the smile that seemed contagious to everybody in the room. She was exciting, to say the least.

"Roc," said Wild Boy Reed after gathering himself, "...tell Aunt Ginny to make another plate."

And she did. Five minutes later, Angel was eating oxtails from a plate in front of her too.

"Ummm...this is good," she said, following Wild Boy Reed's lead on how to eat them, using not only the fork but using two greasy fingers as well to pick up each piece separately, taking meat off the bone in one mouthful after another.

Ray and I had a drink and watched, and then Roc and I talked for a while, waiting patiently until the two were finished eating.

"How was it? Did you like it?" Wild Boy Reed asked

afterward, liking the idea of Angel's courage in sharing such an exotic meal of something she'd never had before.

"Whew...yes, that was delicious," she said, depositing the dirty napkin over the bones and scraps that were left on the plate.

"Can we come back for dinner?" she asked, though, looking over at me, beaming from ear to ear, which made everybody else smile and laugh again too.

"Sure," I said, just to play along.

An hour later, Wild Boy Reed was signing a contract. He got the same ten million dollars that Big Money Records was offering, but with a one million dollar signing bonus, *along with a few other perks and incentives; of course,* I explained and told him.

And not only that...as the leading representative for Mix Master Productions, I was able to guarantee the entire sum of the contract.

"...as long as all the obligations are met and upheld within the five-year period that we've planned for," I told him, making it all plain and clear.

Wild Boy Reed agreed and was eager to sign.

"Welcome to the family," I said about the Mix Master Productions company.

After calling and faxing Giorgio a signed copy of the contract and after writing out a one million dollar check to Jean Claude Mathurin, aka Wild Boy Reed, who had suddenly become a multimillionaire, then everything was finally finalized.

The five of us smiled and shook hands all around.

"You know where to find me if you're ever down here again and wanna have another good meal," Wild Boy Reed told Angel as we were leaving.

"Yep, I sure do...and thanks," said Angel, following me towards the door.

Roc, who'd just gotten off the phone, met us there at the door.

"Those two Philadelphia clowns from the FBI are back, and they're followin' you two again."

"And there's also a silver Grand Marquis followin' behind them. Two more men are in it, and they're with the FBI as well."

I wanted to know, so I asked, "What makes you say that? How can you be so sure?"

I also wondered, *"Two cars with men in them from the FBI? Why?"*

"Believe me, I know what I'm talkin' about. It's my job," Roc said in a way that looked and sounded convincing enough to make me think, *"He really does know what the hell he's doin' and talkin' about."*

"There must be somethin' incriminating as hell in that phone of yours," he said, looking at Angel, "...somethin' that can send their asses to jail more than likely, otherwise they wouldn't be on you so hard," he said, being very serious in his attempt to explain things. While Angel and Wild Boy Reed ate, I told Roc as much as I knew about what happened the night before when the two FBI special agents showed up at the club unannounced. I even told him about Special Agent Maria Lopez Montero's visit to the hotel.

"Special Agent Lopez Montero is good people, she honest, and she's fair, somebody you can trust. But still, if I were you, I'd be very careful. The rest of these guys might not be on the up and up at all," he said, warning us both.

"Watch yourself, you hear?" he said before opening the door to let us out.

"Oh, don't worry, I plan to," was my nonchalant response, something I said just to sound cool and somewhat in control of the situation. Even so, deep down inside, I was now a nervous wreck and worried as hell...*even about somethin' so simple as walkin' out the damn door to leave.*

I thought about calling Special Agent Lopez Montero to ask her about what the hell was going on. I didn't, though, and managed to maintain a level of cool and gallantry that got Angel and me safely outside to the SUV. But I would most definitely be on guard and watching things a lot more closely from that point on.

Chapter 35

The whole time after driving away, I kept a constant watch in the rearview mirror. I easily spotted the two special agents from Philadelphia, the tall white guy and the muscle-bound black guy who was driving. They were a few cars behind us riding in a black Crown Vic.

The silver Grand Marquis that Roc had told us about was a little more difficult and further back. But eventually, I spotted them, too, about half a mile or so behind us. It was hard to see the two who were inside of it; whether they were black or white, male or female, all I saw were two heads.

But then, although the sun had already made its usual evening dip westward towards California and all the other major cities of the western hemisphere, it still left a blinding light that covered most of I-95, making it hard to see too far in front of or behind you.

"It'll be dark soon," I was thinking, realizing the bright light was just a curtain call and final performance of Mother Nature saying goodbye while turning the bright lights of the day into a

most anticipated darkened night.

"What now?" I wondered about the two cars of men from the FBI who were still following me.

"What's next?" I wondered, realizing if a move was to be made against us, it would surely be made at night...*in the cover of darkness.*

In each moment, the sun's disappearing act progressed faster and made it so I couldn't even see them anymore, the two cars that were no doubt still following us. What made it so hard was that all the other headlights of other cars were mixing in together, making it hard to tell one set of headlights from the other.

"I'm wastin' my time tryin' to see 'em in the rearview mirror," I thought, driving along, wondering if I should get off the Interstate or not.

"Probably not." I decided while changing lanes to go around an eighteen-wheeler. Several cars behind me changed lanes too, and they were all going around the eighteen-wheeler.

"You alright?" Angel asked, with a worried look on her face as well.

"Probably because of me...if I'm worried and afraid, she's definitely gonna be worried and afraid," I thought privately.

"Yeah, I'm fine," I said, lying to make things better for her. But it didn't work.

"Are they still behind us?" she asked, just to let me know she knew what was going on too.

It made no sense to keep lying, so I told her the truth.

"I'm not sure anymore...one set of headlights looks no different from the other," which they didn't.

Angel surprised me when she turned and, from the backseat, grabbed the Faraday bag with the phone inside of it.

"I got an idea how we might lose 'em," she said, now with the phone in her hand.

A moment or two later, she had the speaker phone on so I could hear the call she was making.

"Yeah...who dis'?" the husky voice on the other end asked after only the first ring.

"Nigga...who do you think it is," said Angel, in a tone of voice I hadn't heard her use before, one mixed with Ebonics and a certain level of street slang only those from the hood would use. "...and I'll be your worst fuckin' nightmare if you don't act right," she said and told the person on the other end, who was now laughing and laughing hard and loudly.

"Angel? Bitch...where you been!?!" he asked, as if he'd just found his long-lost best friend.

"Where you at?" was the next thing he wanted to know.

"Not too far, and headin' your way."

"Bet...come on...I got a lil' somethin' for you when you get here then."

"No, listen. I need a favor."

"Okay, sure...what you need?" the guy said, with a sound in his voice that made me think he would do whatever she asked him to do.

"I'm ridin' with a friend. We're headed back to Jacksonville, but we got these undercovers on our ass."

"Say no more," the guy told her as if he knew exactly what she wanted and needed him to do.

"Bring 'em by the spot; you know where I'm at. They won't be followin' y'all for much longer, I guarantee it."

"Okay, baby...and thanks. I owe you one."

"You owe me nothin', we folks, and I'll die for mine."

"Just bring your ass own," he said and hung up while laughing at her again.

"That's Javonte, my play brother. His sister and I grew up together and were the best of friends."

"She passed away a few years ago, but Javonte and I are still closer than ever," said Angel, explaining things.

Javonte Carter, aka *Nukey* to those who knew him on the streets, was a five-foot-five-inch *Boar hog* who had for years maintained a strong hold on the streets of West Palm Beach. Him and his crew sold cocaine, crack, heroin, marijuana, meth, x-pills, and whatever else they thought they could sell to make money.

He was originally from Jacksonville, where he grew up the youngest and the only boy in a fatherless household with five sisters.

Their mother was strung out on crack, which was how Javonte learned about it and got the idea of selling drugs. The dope boys on the street where they lived used to get all his mother's extra money...*and the bill money sometimes, too, along with everybody else's money who wanted to get high.*

Javonte saw it as a way out and, at an early age, went into business for himself, taking on his mother and all of her friends as the first faithful customers.

Angel and Tameka, one of Javonte's older sisters, met in junior high school, where they immediately became the best of friends. Angel ran away twice and went to live with them in Jacksonville both times. Once, when Angel ran away, Javonte brought some beer home, and the three of them got drunk together. After Tameka passed out, Javonte and Angel had sex, a first for both of them. Turns out Javonte was well endowed and hurt Angel badly, rupturing the virgin walls inside of her...*and she wouldn't stop bleeding.*

Pete, who wasn't too fond of Angel having such black friends, ended up being called anyway, and it was he and Bobby who came and got her. She spent two days in the hospital with Pete and Bobby right there beside her.

Javonte was eventually chased out of Jacksonville but landed squarely on his feet there in West Palm Beach with cousins who lived there already. A year later, his mother died from an overdose. His two older sisters were married, and two of his other sisters had joined the Navy. But Tameka...she was killed by a jealous lover, a guy Javonte eventually came back and found and killed as well.

He stayed in jail for two years, charged with murder, but was eventually released when witnesses started disappearing, and other witnesses started refusing to testify in fear they might disappear too.

The whole time, Angel faithfully sent money and came to visit.

"I'll never forget what you did for me," he told her after they finally released him.

"We're family. I'd do it again if I had to," Angel told him, and she meant it. They seemed to have a bond that would never be broken.

Chapter 36

"Angel...you sure you know what you're doin'?" I asked, now scared and nervous as hell again.

"Of course I do," she lied, telling me, only hoping things would turn out right. "...just get off here, at this exit," she then said, directing me off to the 49th Street exit there in West Palm Beach.

We made a right on 49th, went past the 49th Street Flea Market, and about a mile further down, we made another right on Central Avenue. Years had passed since the last time I'd been to West Palm Beach, but I remembered enough to know that where we were headed was towards the rough side of town, nowhere near Donald Trump's house.

We rode through three major intersections before Angel directed me to turn left.

"Here... turn left at this street," she said, looking around, sitting up in the seat to be sure she'd gotten it right.

"Yeah, this is it," she said once I'd made the turn.

The houses I saw didn't look so bad, and neither did the neighborhood. The lawns were all mowed, the cars parked in driveways looked decent, and the street was without litter or any riff-raff or mayhem from people standing around. Actually, everything seemed awfully quiet and peaceful. But that was in the first block.

"Keep goin'," Angel told me after we'd stopped at the first stop sign.

In the rearview mirror, I noticed a set of headlights turning in on the street, coming behind us.

"Here they come," I said, suddenly feeling quite nervous again.

"Just keep goin'," said Angel, as if she was now the one in charge, which she was.

I was thinking, *"Somehow, whether we get outta this or not is gonna depend on her and her friends and what happens next."*

"Here... slow down," she said before yelling, "STOP!!!"

And when we did, a group of guys came out from between the sides of two houses.

Angel rolled down the window and immediately started giggling.

"Look at you," she said when one guy came over and stuck his head inside the window.

"Muah," she said after throwing both arms around his neck and kissing him. I immediately became jealous.

"Nigga, don't be kissin' all over me," he said, not meaning it, though. I could tell by the way he smiled and looked all happy. In a way, it made me feel good too, and envious to see two people so happy and glad about seeing one another.

The happy reunion wouldn't last for very long, though.

"Nuke," I heard one of the other guys standing behind him say.

I looked in the rearview mirror and saw that the set of headlights behind us had passed the stop sign and was now coming closer, approaching us. There was also a second set of headlights turning in on the first block.

"Okay...y'all go on and get outta here. We got you," he said, looking not only at Angel but over at me too. The smile was suddenly gone, and the kind face had turned sour, replaced with a look that was now dead serious.

"Go ahead, go," he said, stepping away from the car.

Next, as we were leaving, he pulled out a cell phone and started barking orders.

"Keep goin' straight," Angel told me after I'd gotten to the next stop sign.

A look in the rearview mirror showed the quiet, once empty two blocks of the neighborhood were suddenly now filled with cars and people. Cars had pulled out from driveways to block the paths, front and back, of both cars coming behind us. And all of a sudden, I heard loud rap music and saw people come out from everywhere and start dancing in the streets.

"They won't be coming after us for a while," I said, smiling inside.

"Nope, they sure won't," said Angel, after turning around in the seat to look out the back window, smiling at what she saw.

We were both relieved.

Hell, I was thinking, *"...the next time I see Nuke, I might even give him a big hug too."*

Chapter 37

"Dillon Edward Olamay? Governor Dillon Edward Olamay?" the men from the FBI said and asked while standing at the front entrance of the governor's mansion.

"As if they don't already know who I am," the governor was thinking.

They did know who he was, but the whole approach was just a formality in the legal process of what was about to happen next.

"Sir, we have a warrant for your arrest. You have the right to remain silent. Anything you say can and will be used against you in a court of law."

The governor had already gotten word on what was about to happen, and he had prepared himself. His chief of staff was present, as well as three of the best lawyers in town, two of whom were personal friends.

And, of course, Elaine was there, to gawk mostly and to laugh while making fun of him. But the joke would be on her too when the director of the FBI stepped to her and said, "Elaine...about those ten million dollars...the money you got from the governor. We're gonna need that back, that is, if you don't wanna go to jail with him."

"But Marty," the First Lady said, starting to protest, "Dillon and I are married, you know. So, it's actually my money anyway."

"Okay, well, get it in probate, or divorce court, either or, I don't care which. But in the meantime, I want it back," said the director, unwilling to argue about it, making his decision final.

Those who were listening thought, *"The money could be gotten in divorce court, maybe. Probate court was for when somebody died,"* which hadn't happened yet; the governor was still alive.

When the director thought the First Lady had taken too long in answering, he called over a female FBI agent who'd been brought along just for this occasion.

"Stroud," he said, which was the special agent's last name.

While walking towards the First Lady, Special Agent Stroud, with a serious look on her face, immediately produced a set of handcuffs.

"Okay, alright...I just need to go back to that God-awful bank again. I'll have the bank manager draw up a check."

"Stroud, escort the First Lady down to the Bank of Philadelphia. Take three other agents with you, and be sure to have them cover both entrances while the First Lady goes in to get the money back."

"And if she gives you any trouble, put the cuffs on her."

"Yes sir," said Special Agent Stroud, speaking her first words since being addressed. Before then, being the smart ass that she was, Elaine Olamay wondered if Special Agent Stroud was mute or not.

***

Outside, an area had been cordoned off where the press was being allowed to wait. One reporter yelled out a question, asking, "GOVERNOR OLAMAY...DID YOU KILL RYAN MITSER!?!"

Another reporter yelled out and asked, "GOVERNOR OLAMAY...DID YOU HIRE THOSE TWO SPECIAL AGENTS FROM THE FBI TO DO YOUR DIRTY WORK!?!"

The governor was clearly bothered by this, questions slandering the good name and reputation that had taken him years to build and make good, earning him the utmost respect.

"FUCK YOU!!!" was what he wanted, and seemed tempted to yell back and say.

And then, after they'd gotten him in the car, handcuffed, and taken into custody like a common criminal, he looked out the back window and saw one particular face that stood out from all the rest.

"Fuckin' bitch," he said after seeing the smug look on Kadisha Muhammad's ebony, brown-skinned, pretty face.

"I bet she's happy."

And she was happy to see justice finally being done.

Chapter 38

"Honey...where are you?" Adele asked when Angel answered the phone.

"We're on the way. Trent had business to take care of before we left Miami. A couple more hours, we should be there, though."

"Okay, but we left the hospital. So come to the house; we're waiting."

"Okay, it shouldn't be too much longer before we get there. I'll see you then." I noticed Angel mentioned nothing about the stop we made in West Palm Beach, and once we got there, I wouldn't either.

"We're goin' back to my uncle's house on the beach. I wanna go back the same way we left, through Old Man Gulley's orange grove. And we can leave the SUV parked on the beach just in case those guys from the FBI ever come back."

"Okay," I said, in total agreement, and left it at that, with Angel and I riding along silently, caught in our own private thoughts.

Besides everything else that had happened so far on our trip to Florida, an announcement on the radio gave us even more to think about.

"Earlier today, Governor Dillon Olamay of Pennsylvania was arrested on charges of murder. Details of the arrest are sketchy and being withheld by those in charge due to an ongoing investigation, but word is the First Lady was somehow involved, as well special agents of the FBI. We haven't been told for sure, but from my understanding, other arrests are expected."

Immediately, Angel and I looked over at each other and thought about the two special agents who had been following us the whole time.

"Wow...I wonder if those two had anything to do with it." Angel asked, sharing what the both of us had been thinking.

"Yeah, they probably do. And I bet that phone has something to do with it too."

***

Earlier in the day, while Angel and I were with Wild Boy Reed and his friends in Little Haiti, Special Agent Lopez Montero had a visit with Harry Burgess. She wanted to know about The Ghost.

Harry's wife had been called and then flown in, right after the accident happened. She was there in the room with him.

"Mrs. Burgess, would you mind excusing us for a moment while I speak to your husband?" she asked, cutting to the chase, ready to ask questions.

After the wife was gone, Special Agent Lopez Montero got right to it.

"Where is he, Harry?" she asked, taking a seat in a chair right beside the bed where Harry's wife had been sitting only moments ago.

"Your brother...where is he?" she asked again, watching Harry stall, trying to think of what to say.

"The C Company in Afghanistan. My husband...he was once part of it too. He told me about a guy they called *The Ghost,* an expert in killing...a killing machine. A guy who could get in and out undetected, which was how he got the name. He seemed able to do the impossible, get in and out of places and situations when nobody else could. In the last mission, however, the situation seemed impossible again, and it proved to be that it was. They were supposedly all killed, including my husband. In the end, though, the body of all of them were recovered and returned home, all except one, the body belonging to Alexander K. Burgess, aka The Ghost, your older brother, Harry."

"Now, I know you've been in contact with him. That's how he knows so much about the case that you're on, a case contracted to him by the Pennsylvania Governor's chief of staff, William 'Bill' Gray, who was Alex's best friend all through high school."

"Governor Olamay has been arrested and taken into custody. Bill Gray will be too. But now I'm tryin' to save the life of a young lady your brother plans to kill."

"Come on, Harry. You've got daughters. Would you want them hunted down and killed senselessly? No, you wouldn't," said Special Agent Lopez Montero, playing on the soft side of Harry Burgess, who seemed about ready to cry.

"And it's ironic because the whole time, 'Uncle Alex' has been depositing money in an account set up by him as a college fund for three other young ladies, the three nieces he loves so much."

Special Agent Lopez Montero paused for a moment to catch a breath and to allow everything she said to sink in on the conscience side of Harry's thinking.

"Okay...I've told you what I know," she said, continuing. "Now tell me what you know."

Alexander Burgess was only older than Harry by two years, and the two looked so much alike that people sometimes thought they were twins too.

That's why Pete thought Harry was The Ghost. One of the young men of C Company who was killed happened to be the son of Pete's cousin in Boston. After the funeral, Pete was shown pictures and was told that the only body not recovered was that belonging to the red-headed kid in the picture, a kid all the other guys in C Company called The Ghost.

Chapter 39

"Trent...can we stop? I need to use the bathroom," Angel said, touching me on the arm, which made chills run throughout my whole body. I loved it when she touched me.

"Yeah...there's a rest area comin' up. I was thinkin' about the same thing."

Five minutes later, I was standing at a urinal, relieving myself. I heard it when the door opened behind me, but I paid it no mind, thinking it was just somebody else coming in to use the bathroom too. But the guy who came in was Special Agent Wheeler, and he had a blackjack in one of his hands. The next thing I knew, I was being hit hard over the head. It hurt so bad I thought I would die. And then I heard gunshots and a scream.

"Angel," I said, holding on to what little consciousness I had left.

The roadblock that Angel's friend, Nuke, had put up for us in West Palm Beach was only a temporary fix. Actually, Wheeler drove up on the curb and hit a guy who got in the way of him driving across somebody's lawn in his attempt to go around it coming after us.

The silver Grand Marquis was the only one of the two vehicles held up for any surmountable amount of time until cars from the West Palm Beach Sheriff's Department started showing up. But Special Agents Wheeler and Marks, they'd caught up and had been following behind us the whole time.

After hearing the shots that were fired, Wheeler left me and ran out of the bathroom, and then I heard more shots fired.

"Angel," I said again, still with very little consciousness.

I was barely able to make it to the bathroom door, but when I did, even more shots were fired, with one bullet barely missing my head but with another hitting me high in the shoulder. By chance, I was able to make out the figure firing the shots...a guy about six feet in height, two hundred pounds maybe, wearing a dark-colored hoodie. What stood out about him, though, was that he had curly red hair under the hoodie...*The Ghost.*

I fell as if I were dead, which might've been the only reason he stopped shooting at me. Wheeler was already dead, laying on the ground right there in front of me. And so was Marks...I could only see one leg sticking halfway out the lady's room, but to me, it was obvious the condition he'd been left in.

I watched as the hooded assassin left, walking away as cool as a guy going for a late-night walk. And then he was gone, disappearing in the darkness.

"Angel," I said, with just enough energy to stand and walk. I lost that, too, once I stepped over Marks and made it inside the ladies' room. Angel was lying there on the floor.

"...dead too, obviously," I thought, with the reality of it crushing me.

"Oh, God...no," I said, barely in a whisper, from being barely able to speak and get the words out. The only thing that seemed to want to come out were tears. I couldn't stop myself from bawling, crying uncontrollably.

"NNOOOO!!!" I finally yelled out and shouted. It felt as if my whole world had ended, and it had; life as I knew it was over.

Suddenly I started remembering things, things about Angel...

"Hey...turn that thing down," she said about the radio,

"Oh, and on the way, I need for you to stop in Richmond and in St. Augustine, just south of Jacksonville," she said after only being on the passenger side of the SUV for thirty seconds.

These were things I was starting to recollect, remembering about her.

"Tell me about you, Trent Walker, and how you became to be such a successful writer and record producer. Start from the beginning. You know, like, 'I was born in...' from that beginning."

Everything I remembered crushed me even more.

And then I thought about Adele and the family there in St. Augustine waiting for me to bring her home.

"We're goin' back to my uncle's house on the beach," she'd told me, "I wanna go back the way we left, through Old Man Gulley's orange grove."

"Okay," I said, all choked up inside with tears in my eyes, as if the words I recalled were just spoken to me by her. I was delirious, unable to think or speak clearly.

Regardless of being shot or anything else, the mission now was to get Angel home.

"Come on, baby, let me help you," I said, scrambling over to get beside her. And then, while enduring the pain and using all the strength I could muster, I put my arms beneath her and picked Angel up off the ground.

By the time I got her in the back seat and closed the door of the SUV, the silver Grand Marquis was pulling up. Seeing that I was shot, both Special Agents quickly unholstered their weapons and took off running toward the bathrooms.

I didn't bother to wait; as a matter of fact, they weren't somebody I wanted to trust either. So, when they took off running towards the bathroom, I got in the SUV and took off too.

"I'm takin' you home, baby," I said after I'd gotten back on I-95 and had time to look towards the backseat again where I'd put Angel's beautiful dead body.

"I'm takin' you home where you'll be safe."

Chapter 40

A storm was brewing, and clouds were moving a lot faster than usual, but people couldn't see it because of how dark it was outside. And over the ocean waters of the South Atlantic, the fog was gathering and moving inland towards the shore. Every now and then, a strike of lightning would light the darkened sky, but otherwise, nobody was able to notice the gateway to heaven that was opening.

"Go towards the light, my child. When you see it, go towards it," said one of the acolytes, the hundred- and forty-seven-year-old woman at her place there under the big oat tree on the outskirts of Richmond, at Adele's old farmhouse. The woman was watching as if she could see everything that was happening to us in Florida. And she could, thanks to her intuition and a magical gift to see things from a distance.

The light the woman mentioned were the strikes of lightning that were becoming more and more fierce and intense the further I drove north towards Flagler Beach and St. Augustine. At one point,

I even thought I heard Angel stir in the back seat behind me from being ready to get there...*or maybe it's just what I sensed.*

At the house in St. Augustine, Adele wept and cried like a baby, expressing deep sorry and passion, not because Pete had died but because she feared the worst for Angel...*it was as if she knew already.*

Aunt Irene and Bobby tried consoling her, but how could they when they didn't even understand not only what was happening but also the significance of why it was happening? Angel was about to be born again, not in the earthly sense of flesh and blood, but spiritually in a whole different universe of do-gooders. God had chosen Angel long ago, and now he had sent for her to come home and join him in the kingdom.

Although, as much as it hurt to lose Angel, the tears Adele cried were also tears of joy, joy because she knew Angel was going to a much better place and that one day she would be joining him too.

Chapter 41

I was bleeding and losing blood too fast.

"I'm not gonna make it," I thought, fearing I might pass out while driving. *"...before I can even get where I was going."*

And then I saw an exit for Flagler Beach; it was two miles ahead of us. And better yet, I then thought I recognized the next exit as the exit I'd used to get on I-95 when Angel and I were leaving Flagler Beach on our way to Miami. I was wrong in both cases and was suffering badly from illusions.

Where I ended up getting off the Interstate was five miles and three exits before the exit where I was actually supposed to have gotten off. But it felt as if I was being directed and pulled in the direction I was going as if I had no other choice.

And at the end of the road that I'd gotten off on and driven down, there was indeed an orange grove, just not the orange grove that belonged to Mr. Gulley.

After driving down a dirt road and path through the orange

grove, there I was, back on the beach again, but miles away from Angel's uncle's house.

The tide was going out, which made the shoreline a lot wider than if the tide was coming in, which made me drive a lot further out too. But while driving along, consciousness seemed to be leaving, forcing me to stop, put the SUV in park, and ultimately turn it off, thinking I might only need to nap for a while.

Who knows when the fog came, but the next thing I knew, it was there. It had me and the SUV totally engulfed. At the same time, lightning struck harder than ever and was louder than I'd ever heard it before.

And then there were people all around the SUV, but they weren't there for me. They were there for Angel and the soul that was still trapped inside her body. Angel stirred again, and this time I was sure of it. She stirred and stirred until, finally, the soul separated itself and allowed the people around us to carry it away. The last thing I saw was an opening in the fog leading up to what I guessed was the gateway to heaven. That's where Angel's soul was being taken.

The next morning, I woke up without a memory and worried about whether I would drown or not. After driving further ashore, and after the police got there, Angel's body was taken to the morgue, and I was taken to the hospital, but not before it started to rain, and a rainbow appeared in the sky... Angel was saying goodbye.

Eventually, Adele and the rest of Angel's family got to the hospital, and so did Special Agent Lopez Montero. Nobody seemed mad or upset with me. They were more relieved and gladder that I'd survived, especially Adele.

Epilogue

"I know about Marks and Wheeler...the two corrupt geniuses from Philly. I was gonna arrest their ass anyway before somebody shot and killed them. So, as far as I'm concerned, good riddance," said Special Agent Maria Lopez Montero about the two now-deceased special agents.

The FBI special agent, after being sworn in as Chief, was now officially the one in charge of the Miami/South Florida area FBI office. It was made official the day she revealed who The Ghost was. He was still on the loose, avoiding capture, but now, thanks to Special Agent Lopez Montero, the FBI, Interpol, and the rest of the world knew exactly who he was.

It was then that she took the cuffs off.

"You were never under arrest; these were put on just so you would stop running from us."

"By the way...the men following you in the silver, Grand Marquis...I sent them, and they worked for me. I sent them to protect you. But as it turned out, fate took a nasty course, and unfortunately, Angel Clark was killed anyway."

"But from what I understand, things haven't turned out to be so bad after all," she said, looking up at the smiling face of Adele, who was standing right there beside me.

***

The memory of my entire life might've been wiped away, but not my desire for love. I could only hope that, in time, I would regain some kind of memory or recognition of who I once was. But in the meantime, Giorgio had sent severance pay of five million dollars from Mix Masters and had wished Adele and me the best of luck.

If you're wondering how I was able to tell such a story without a memory, then wonder more about the mystery of magic. Actually, it was done with me being under hypnosis, in a subconscious state. Before being exonerated, the FBI insisted it be done. Otherwise, without them hypnotizing me, I still wouldn't remember.

And now, with that done, *I plan to spend the rest of my life making new memories with the woman I love.*

***

That night at the tree, the tree of life, a meeting was being held in honor of the person we'd all lost and loved. Only this time, the leader was present. He'd come down out of the heavens that night just to join them.

"It was indeed a joyous night after all."

The leader was a man with golden skin filled with many years of wear and tear.

"It's like he'd lived forever."

And he had hair that was like wool, Lamb's wool, but white like snow. He also seemed to be a Hispanic and was known simply as Jesús.

The end

Regardless of religion or social belief, we need to believe in *something*, preferably something spiritual, something of God. Otherwise, if we don't believe in *something*, then we leave ourselves vulnerable and susceptible to falling for anything.

If you enjoyed or have an opinion otherwise about what you've read, please leave a review on Amazon. I read every review, and they help new readers discover my books.

Thanks, and God bless.

www.ingramcontent.com/pod-product-compliance
Lightning Source LLC
LaVergne TN
LVHW061046070526
838201LV00074B/5197